CONVERGENCE BY: LAYLA M. GATLIN

CONVERGENCE BY: LAYLA M. GATLIN

LAYLA GATLIN

Special thanks to:
All the nurses, doctors, teachers, and
plant experts I reached out to with
questions during the writing process. I
cannot name everyone by name but I
appreciate you all.

Written by Layla M. Gatlin
Cover by Kayla N. Todd

© 2024
IngramSparks Publishing

Prologue:

Doctor James Overton sauntered through the front door of his modest country home and kicked off his work shoes. His feet were blistered from walking all day but he barely noticed it as his thoughts drifted back to work. He had just finished his twenty hour shift at NASA's research and development lab at the Johnson Space Center that day. It's not abnormal for him to work long hours but the last few days he had barely gotten four hours of sleep between shifts. The physical effects of exhaustion were nothing, however, compared to the emotional stress over the thought of what might happen... of what could be coming...

"James honey? Is that you?"

His wife Maryann leaned around the corner of the kitchen door frame. When she saw that it was indeed her husband she rushed over to him and embraced him. "I'm so glad you're home. When do you have to be back?" Her sad eyes seemed to beg him to say something he unfortunately couldn't.

"4am." He avoided eye contact with her when he said it. She glanced back at the clock above the kitchen door and moaned.

"It's 11 already! That's even less time than yesterday!" Her grip seemed to tighten even more and he grimaced at the thought of how much it hurt her for him to leave. But he has no choice. He's doing it for them...

Upon the thought, as if on cue, his 13 year old daughter Samantha comes thudding down the stairs.

"Dad! You're home! Guess what happened at school today! So there's this guy in my social studies class and we got paired for a project and..."

"Um, Sam honey... I'm sorry sweetheart but I have to be back at work in just a few hours so I need to get to bed..." He pulled away from his wife and headed towards Samantha. He kissed her on the forehead as he walked past, up the stairs to his and his wife's bedroom.

Maryann gave Samantha a sad look and mouthed 'I'm sorry'. Samantha blinked back tears and stormed up the stairs to her room, slamming the door behind her. James could hear the door thud from down the hall as he climbed into bed. He gritted his teeth together to keep from becoming emotional. He knows his family is hurting and it kills him. He would give anything for things to go back to the way they were... and he hope's they someday will... but they definitely won't if he doesn't keep working as he has been.

'It's for them. They don't understand. But I have to protect them...' he reaffirmed himself as he curled up under the blanket and drifted off to sleep.

Chapter One

"Did you tell your parents about the project?" Shane asks as I take my seat next to him at the table and pull out my social studies textbook. The white board at the front of the room says to turn to page 92 and read the chapter on civil justice warriors to prepare for our projects. I flip to it but I can't concentrate on the words right now.

"Not exactly... I mean, I told mom. Dads... busy." I grind my teeth a little at the thought and Shane instantly noticed my mood.

"I'm sorry Sam. Well, maybe your mom will tell him?" He leans forward to try to see my face which is staring blankly down at the book in front of me. His shaggy dark brown hair is almost long enough to cover his wavy blue eyes when he leans forward. He doesn't usually let it get this long. I kind of like the long hair on him though... I think it makes him look even cuter...

Yeah, I have a crush on Shane. We've become good friends this semester having this class together. I never knew I could have so much in common with a boy. And he's so funny and understanding and stuff so it's hard not to fall for him. Of course, I'd never tell him I'm crushing on him! I don't want to lose him as a friend if he thinks that's too weird... I'm just hoping maybe one day he will feel the same for me and tell me first so I don't have to be the initiator.

"Thanks, yeah maybe. I don't know that she sees him much more than me though."

He is just about to respond when our teacher announces it's time to start class and we straighten up and pull our textbooks closer. Trying to look like we actually did what we were supposed to. Well, Shane might have actually.

"We can talk more later okay?" He whispers to me. "Okay. For sure!" I nod.

"Samantha Overton, is there something you'd like to share with the class?" Our teacher Mrs. Francis questions.

My face turns bright red and I sink down in my chair a bit shaking my head.

"Okay well let's focus on social studies then shall we?" I nod and make a point not to look at anyone after that. When the bell rings I'm more than thankful for it to be time to go and I dart out as fast as I can.

Mom picks me up out front after school as she does everyday. I slide into the open van door and pull it shut behind me. I used to ride the bus. I didn't mind riding the bus cause I got to spend more time with Shane but I think mom thinks she has to spend more time with me since dad isn't ever home anymore. It's like she's trying to make up for him or something. But then I also think maybe she's just lonely too and needs me... so I don't complain about being a car rider.

I stare out the window as we drive through town. Where we live is outside of the city limits and is more secluded than the rest of the town. I'd say it's out in the country but really the whole state of Texas is pretty much 'out in the country'. Well, aside from Dallas and the other few big city areas.

When we get home mom makes dinner and we sit together at the table. Dad isn't home yet. No surprise. He probably won't be in till super late again and will probably have to be right back at work before I'm even awake for school in the morning.

At about 9 o'clock mom gives me the 'bedtime look'. I'm pretty much allowed to stay up as late as I want but I have to be doing something quiet in my room, like reading or drawing or something. So around 9 mom usually expects me to head that way.

I smile and hug her goodnight before trotting up the stairs to my room. Plopping in bed I decide to go ahead and get some sleep tonight. We are supposed to start our project tomorrow and I'm so excited. The sooner I get to sleep the sooner it'll be tomorrow. I get comfortable and pull the cover up under my chin but just as I go to close my eyes I hear the front door downstairs open. I bolt upright in bed and listen.

"James? Why are you home so early?" Mom's voice was barely audible from the living room but I heard it.

I jump out of bed and start to run downstairs but suddenly think better of it. They will probably stop talking if I come down... Maybe I can sneak down and eavesdrop...

I pull on a pair of socks so my feet won't stick to the wood floor and give me away. Then I slowly twist the doorknob and pull it open, careful not to let it creak. My feet slide across the floor as I make my way, pressed against the wall, down the stairs. I stop on the step before last and listen carefully.

I can hear them in the living room whispering and I lean forward a bit more trying to strain to hear.

"An asteroid? Like from space?" Mom's voice sounds confused.

"Well, yes but it's going to break apart into 3 pieces. One big, two smaller."

"And they are gonna hit earth?"

"We can't be 100% certain. It has already changed course several times without warning. But we know either all three pieces will barely miss earth or all three will hit it. I've been working tirelessly to find a solution or at least confirm which path it will take but there seems to be nothing that can be done on either account." Dads voice wavers as if he's trying to conceal his fear. Hearing my dad so afraid actually causes my stomach to become upset and I grab it.

"So what can be done?" The quiver in mom's voice makes my stomach even more upset. I might throw up...

"Nothing. We just have to wait. They will sound the alarm if it's going to collide and we will have about a half an hour at that point to get to the center where they have chambers set up underground for emergencies. The chambers will be the best chance anyone has. If the alarm doesn't sound it means the asteroids will pass by us and every-thing will be okay."

"This is happening tonight?! Why didn't you tell me sooner?!"

"Nothing was, or is, certain and I didn't want to worry yall. But it is what it is... I'm gonna wait up for a while. You should try to get some sleep."

"No, I'll stay up with you. But you should probably go see if Sam is up and kiss her goodnight... if everything does go crazy tonight it may be the last chance you get... don't leave things like they've been with her..."

"You're right. I'll head up there now and see." The sound of the couch creaking from the release of weight sent my legs a movin.

I darted up the stairs as quickly as I could without thudding and bolted into my room and straight towards my bed. Covering up as quick as I can I pretend to be asleep. When I hear dad's breathing in the doorway I clench my eyes shut even tighter.

"Samantha... you awake?" His voice sounds hopeful and I try to hold back a tear as I keep up my silent charade. I can hear his footsteps coming closer and it takes everything in me not to flinch when he kisses my forehead.

"I love you Samantha. I'm so sorry it hasn't seemed like it lately... but I love you and your mother more than anything in the world. I pray you know that... Goodnight sweetheart..."

As his footsteps fade away and my door clicks shut I finally allow myself to break down. That night I cried myself to sleep...

Chapter Two

Lights flashing outside my window wake me from a dead sleep. Screams can be heard in the distance and I bolt up and run to the window. Down below people are bolting from their houses and running down the street. There's a wreck below and firetrucks and an ambulance are racing towards it. 'Oh, it's just panic from the wreck.' I think as I turn back away from the window. At that moment my parents rush into my room with panic stricken faces and my heart drops.

No... it can't be...

"Sam!" Dad shouts as they rush in. "Grab essentials. Hurry, we don't have much time!"

I do as he says and grab my backpack out of my closet. Mom is already scooping all my clothes out of my drawers and shoving them in a huge duffle bag. I notice she already has a full bag next to her that I assume is their clothes. I grab my cell phone and charger along with my yearbook. I shove them in my backpack which already contains my laptop and journal. I start to follow my parents out the door and down the stairs when I remember something. I race back to my room and grab a small stuffed dog from my bookshelf. It was a gift from my grandparents before they died just a few years ago. I'm too old for stuffed animals but it's sentimental; so I shove it down in my backpack with the rest of my stuff before darting off to meet up with mom and dad again.

Dad rushes us into the car and doesn't bother telling us to buckle up. As soon as all the doors are shut he takes off. My dad is driving like mad and going nearly 25 miles over the speed limit.

But I guess he figures the police are busy with other things and aren't concerned with writing tickets during the apocalypse...

As we speed towards the space center there are lots of people I know panicking in the streets. My heart aches and I yell out, "Dad, we have to bring them with us!"

"We don't have room Sam! Or time!"

"Well we can't just leave them to die!" I insist, yanking my sliding door open as he drives. Mom screams at me and dad slams on the breaks and the car comes to a screeching halt. I leap out and start yelling to everyone to find a vehicle and head to the space center. People begin frantically climbing into cars and onto bicycles and four wheelers and anything else they can find.

The sky suddenly darkens and turns a deep blood red and a chilling wind blows through picking up some small objects and tossing them around. A woman with a young boy, maybe around two years old, runs up to me in tears.

"Please give us a ride! We have no vehicle! Please help us!" She begs as she cradles her son to her chest. The boy is crying uncontrollably, sensing the fear in his mother.

I look back at my parents with a pleading look and dad sighs and nods.

"Of course, but hurry we have to leave now! We don't have much time left!" He waves us in urgently and we all jump in and slam the door closed behind us.

"Thank you! Oh thank you so much!" The woman cries tears of joy and gratitude as she rocks her child in the seat next to me.

Her boy's long blonde hair drapes across his forehead nearly to his eyelids. It kind of reminds me of Shane's... Shane!

I gasp and pull out my phone. Dialing his number as fast as my fingers can move. "Come on... come on..." I whisper to myself as it rings. When the voicemail box comes on it's all I can do not to hyperventilate. Dad glances in the rear view mirror and sees my distressed look as I hit redial.

"Sam? You okay?" He asks, concerned.

"No! I can't get a hold of Shane!" By this point I'm crying. I'm crying so hard I can't see clearly. Everything is a blur and I have a throbbing headache.

"Who's Shane?" Dad asks, confused.

This makes my blubbering even worse and I can't even talk through the sobs. Mom jumps in and tries to reassure me.

"I'm sure Shane and his parents are fine, baby... I called Mrs. Baker last night after your father told me what might happen and warned them to be on their guard and to get to the space center if anything alarming happened."

This actually did calm me a bit. Okay... as long as she warned them, they are probably okay. I'm sure they made it out ... they had to have...

Dad gives mom a look of surprise and she shoots him a weird look back. I'm not sure what to make of it... She's probably mad he doesn't know the Bakers since I talk about them all the time. She

is probably as upset about dad never listening to us as I am. I accept this as a reasonable explanation for the exchange I witnessed and lean my head against the window.

Outside I can hear sirens wailing and car horns honking. The alarm from the space center can be heard faintly through it all. Most people have no idea what's actually going on... they just know the siren is supposed to mean something very bad is coming. It's causing a panic but nobody knows what they are supposed to do to save themselves or their family. It makes me wonder why NASA didn't warn people!

"This is all your fault you know..." I mutter so softly I don't really expect to be heard.

"What was that Sam?" Dad asks.

I blink back more tears and grind my teeth together as I respond, louder this time...

"Just look at this! All these people panicking in the streets! Scared for their lives and for their families and no clue what to do and it's all your fault dad!"

The lady next to me raises an eyebrow and wiggles uncomfortably. I feel bad for her but I'm too angry to think straight.

"SAMANTHA!" Mom yells at me in shock and disapproval.

Dad lays his hand on mom's leg as if to say 'it's okay' and she gets quiet.

"Explain Sam." Dad says softly.

"You could have warned them! You could have made, like, a public announcement days ago on TV or something telling them what might happen and how to handle it if it did... then they wouldn't just be running around like chickens with their heads cut off and probably gonna die!" My face begins to burn as it turns red and my yelling startles the little boy in his mother's arms so that he starts crying again. I instantly feel terrible and sink down lower in my seat.

"I understand your frustration Sam." Dad sighs, "I really do. Believe me I wanted to but my supervisors felt it was best not to cause a panic until we were sure it would even happen. Too many people would have gotten needlessly hurt if it turned out to be a false alarm. So I accepted their decision. Maybe I was wrong, but it's too late now. You can be angry with me if you want. I understand. But I can't change anything now, all I can do is get my family... and others... to safety." He glances in the rearview mirror at the woman and child in the seat next to me. He looks at her with pain in his eyes and I can tell he really is beating himself up over it all. I'm still angry with him. Very angry... but I decide to drop the matter and remain silent for the rest of the ride to the center.

Chapter Three

The Johnson space center parking lot was covered in cars and other modes of transportation. Vehicles lined the streets all the way down the road and sidewalks nearby. Nobody bothered parking sensibly. It looked like everyone just pulled up where they could and abandoned their cars. The stretch is so covered we can't even get through.

"We will have to get out and run!" Dad announces as we all pile out. Mom and I start grabbing our bags and we all make a break for it.

The mother carrying her toddler struggles to keep up with us and I try to slow my pace just a tad to help her out. She doesn't seem to notice but I wouldn't expect her to be focusing on me. We make it to the front doors and dad holds it open as we all rush in. There's a man that flags us to an open latch door in the floor and a staircase that leads down a dimly lit corridor below the building. We don't hesitate to follow it.

The further down we go the noisier it gets. There are people talking and crying and wheezing below, as well as sounds that make me think of some kind of technology beeping and whirring. After a while we see brighter lights up ahead. Soon we come to a metal wall with a large titanium door with a keypad. Dad enters a code and the door clicks unlocked. Dad pushes it open and holds it for us as we all enter.

I take in the scene before me with wide eyes. The room stretches on further than my eye can see, occasionally separated into smaller rooms by thick glass walls and doors. Hundreds of people are huddled together in groups along the walls and throughout the rooms. As we walk through I notice doors along the walls labeled different things like "Pantry", "Cafeteria", "Electric",

"Restrooms/Showers", and "Authorized Personnel Only".

Most of the doors have keypads next to them that apparently can only be opened by NASA employees. The doors labeled "Cafeteria" and "Restrooms/Showers" seem to be the only ones not keypad protected. Towards the back of the room is a set of double doors that are labeled "Living Quarters". These also are not secured by any coded pad. Through them is another huge room, only this one has rows upon rows of bunk beds and cubby holes.

All of the beds appear to have the same blanket and pillow that I suppose NASA had supplied when they created these chambers.

"Throw your bag on a bed that doesn't already have one on it. That'll be yours for the foreseeable future." Dad sounds tired and sad as he says it.

I nod and do as he says, tossing my backpack on the nearest bed that looks untouched. The mom and her little boy sit down on the bed next to mine. She looks around at it and starts to cry. It's then that I notice that they don't have any bags of clothes or toys or anything. Her boy has finally fallen asleep in her arms and she just cradles him and sobs.

It was awkward sitting there watching her cry and I feel bad that she doesn't have any personal belongings with her. Suddenly my mom arrives and sits down beside her, putting her arm around her.

"Hey, it's gonna be alright. I'm Maryann. And this is my daughter Sam," she nods in my direction and I smile nervously, "My husband's name is James. He will be back shortly. What's your name?" Mom's soothing voice seems to calm the young mother down a tad and she wipes her eyes.

"My name is Sara. And this is my son Matthew." She brushes the hair from her sleeping child's eyes as she speaks.

"He's precious. How old is he?" Mom smiles warmly.

"He will be two next month."

"Aww, so it's just the two of you?"

"Yes. My husband..." Her eyes begin to swell with tears again but she blinks them back, "My husband was in the army and he died overseas while deployed on mission six months ago."

Mom's face falls and her shoulders sag slightly, "I'm so sorry for your loss. I'm sure he was a brave and honorable man."

Sara sniffles, "Thank you. He was. I wish he were here now more than anything... he always made me feel so safe. Now Matthew and I only have each other and with this?" She wipes her eyes again and my mom squeezes her gently to reassure her more.

"Well, now you have us. From this point on you and Matthew are part of our family. And we are here for you."

Sara bursts into tears and hugs my mom, thanking her for her kindness. Mom grabs her duffle bag and opens it, pulling out clothes she believes will fit Sara and passing them to her. Matthew starts to stir awake and I get an idea. I pull the stuffed dog out of my backpack and look at it. It means a lot to me but seeing Sara and Matthew with nothing of their own...

"Here, I want Matthew to have this." I hold the dog out to Sara and she looks shocked.

"Oh I... are you sure?" She waits for me to nod before slowly taking the dog from me. "Thank you so much. You all are so sweet and... I just can't thank God enough for bringing you into my life during this time..." her voice is shaky from all the crying and her eyes seem tired and heavy.

Mom notices too, "Sara dear, why don't you and Matthew get some sleep? We should be safe here and it could be a long night. We will wake you if need be."

Sara nods and curls up on the bed with Matthew in her arms. They are both sound asleep in moments. Mom looks at me and nods her head towards the door. I follow her back out into the main auditorium again. Once the double doors close behind us, dad begins coming our way. He has a really concerned look on his face as he motions for us to follow him. Mom grabs my hand and we let dad lead us through the chamber.

At the far right side of the room a huge crowd is forming and dad leads us right into it. On the wall in front of the crowd are dozens of monitors. It becomes eerily quiet as everyone tries to make sense of what they are seeing on the screens. The images look far off and aren't completely clear but I don't think anyone has any trouble understanding what they are looking at.

"These are satellite images from our space station. The images are being relayed in real time..." dad whispers to us, his voice sounds like he's going to throw up. And I wouldn't blame him... in fact a few people nearby go running off with their hands over their mouths to do just that...

We watch as the biggest asteroid hits directly in the center of the eastern hemisphere of the earth. There's a huge wave of colors and fire and smoke... when it all settles there's an audible gasp across the room and a few screams and sobs. Some people leave and run to the restroom or the living quarters. One lady nearby us passes out and a couple people in a medical outfit race to her side.

The image on the screen shows nothing left in the eastern hemisphere. Nothing but molten rock. China, Russia, Europe, Africa, Australia... everything... just gone...

The screens show the smaller asteroids as they enter the atmosphere. When they separated from the main asteroid they flew a lot further off course than the main one.

"They are heading for the US!" Someone screams in the crowd and everyone starts talking and shouting over one another, pointing at the screens and panicking.

Mom and I look at dad, terrified. He looks sad but shakes his head no. I look back at the screen confused. I try to follow the direction of the asteroids and see where else they could be heading.

"No wait! They are gonna miss the US on each side! Look, they will land in the ocean on either side of us! We're safe!" A man at the front of the crowd shouts with glee and points to the monitor as if to show the direction with his hand. There's an audible sigh of relief among the people but dad lets out a low groan.

"What's wrong dad? Isn't that good news?" I ask, unsure why he'd be upset to hear the asteroid will miss the US.

"Samantha... the size of the asteroids... hitting in the ocean at that speed... it'll cause..." Before he can finish his sentence the asteroids make impact and the crowd goes deathly silent as everyone sees exactly what my dad knew all along.

A huge tidal wave forms on both sides of the US and comes rushing directly towards the land. In addition underwater volcanoes are then activated by the change in systemic pressure and begin to erupt all along the coastline. The temperature change and the winds produced by the fall of the asteroids create tornadoes along the coastline as well.

Everyone watches in silence as natural disasters of all kinds begin to tear through the east and west coast of not only the US but also Canada, Mexico, and South America as well.

"Dad, what's going to happen to us?!" I yell through tears in the direction of my father. My shout breaks the silence and everyone turns towards my father as if they suddenly noticed he was wearing a NASA uniform and might have answers.

He looks around nervously at the crowd now staring anxiously at him.

"I... We... I don't know... I'm sorry. The impact from the asteroids will likely destroy all but the middle strip of the western hemisphere... and what's left, us and those to the north and south of us... well we can't be sure what the conditions above ground will be like as of yet. But so long as we can survive down here we are safe. These chambers were specially designed for cataclysmic events. Just... stay here." Dad suddenly looks queasy again and rushes off towards the restrooms. The crowd begins to murmur among themselves and many disperse and head off in different directions.

Mom goes back to the living quarters to check in on Sara and Matthew. I wait where I am for dad to come back out of the restrooms. When he does I try to get his attention and chase after him but he seems distracted and races towards the door labeled "Authorized Personnel Only". He enters a code and quickly slips inside before I can get to him. Just before the door closes I catch a glimpse through the crack of a portion of a room filled with computers and people in NASA uniforms. I consider knocking and seeing if they will open for me but then I decide just to go back with mom, Sara, and Matthew and wait till dad comes back out.

Chapter Four:
(Five Years Later)

My eyes spring open and bolt upright, drenched in sweat. Another nightmare. Five years later and I still get them. I roll off my bunk bed and tip toe towards the main auditorium. Most are still in bed asleep. I probably should be too considering the big day ahead.

It's finally Immersion day. That's what the big NASA guys are calling it anyway. They've been testing the conditions outside for years now with cameras and drones and all kinds of fancy techy stuff. About a year after the impact they injected all of us with a vaccine of sorts they came up with to help our bodies adapt to changes in the environment. Including a surge of radiation emitted by the asteroids when they hit.

Apparently our fancy bunker wasn't as apocalypse ready as the big brained dudes thought. They were afraid radiation would seep in through the ventilation and so they started researching a solution. This injection RAD29-U was created. It literally stands for Radiation Acceleration Deflector and the year it was created, 2029. The serum's main goal is to override our body's defense mechanism to adapt to the changes caused by the radiation instead of fighting it. And it worked. Well, for most of us...

Unfortunately a few of the elderly folks body's didn't respond correctly. It was a very sad time... anyone who dies in the chambers has to be cremated and there isn't a typical funeral... obviously... But we did create a new tradition of sorts to try to help the family grieve. Everyone gathers in the main auditorium and forms a circle to have a moment of silence for the deceased. Some pray to themselves, some cry, some just think good thoughts towards the family. After it's over the family is presented with a metal box with the ashes inside. Someone holds a container of ink and everyone passes by and places a fingerprint on the outside of the box, to show their respects. It's become a very honored tradition for those of us here in the chambers. Especially since we are all so close now... We are all kind of one big family now.

And one race too. That's what I almost forgot to mention... The radiation did end up causing changes to us. One such change was our skin. No matter what race one was before that has all changed. The radiation slowly reworked our DNA to change the pigment of our skin. Thankfully being in the chambers protected us from it being any worse than it was but... everyone in the chambers now has yellow skin. Like a soft sunny yellow. It started slow and we didn't really even notice as it was happening. It really felt like we just woke up and looked in the mirror one day and our skin had completely changed. And it's not the only thing that changed...

The skin was the most noticeable change sure, but we soon realized that everyone's eye colors had changed as well. We all have pink eyes now. Like fuchsia pink. Dad and the other NASA researchers have yet to figure out why pink. The yellow they understand because radiation is itself in physical form a bright green so with us being shielded from the main impact it was dulled to yellow. But they have no idea about the pink eye color thing.

There's also one other thing...

Abilities. I call them superpowers but dad corrects me everytime I do so I mostly keep that word to myself. And no I can't fly or shoot lasers out of my eyes or anything crazy like that. Mostly it's just heightened senses I suppose. We have night vision now and our hearing is phenomenal! There's even a girl here who was born deaf and she can hear again! But like, super softly, as if everyone is whispering. But you should have seen it! She burst into tears randomly one day and was hyperventilating and we were all freaking out trying to figure out what was wrong with her... and she finally just said "I hear you! I hear you all!" It was crazy!

Supposedly some have better smell and are a little stronger too. I haven't noticed those things yet but it didn't all happen at the same time for everyone anyway. It's like we are all constantly changing. Dad thinks our bodies can sense the changes in the atmosphere and stuff outside even though we are down here and it's trying to adapt accordingly. But that's more of a personal theory he has. They haven't proven that exactly.

But that's gonna change soon! Cause they finally, after years of testing and experimenting, are gonna let us out. Dad says their tests have come back completely conclusive that the air outside is livable, at least since we know the vaccine did its job in preventing adverse effects from the radiation. They apparently don't see superpowers and skin color as an adverse effect... I mean I don't guess I do either. Seems like an enhancement, so like, a good thing.

All I know is I can't wait to get out of here! I can't even remember what the sky looks like... I wonder if it even looks the same as before... I guess dad would know but I've never thought to ask him about what the outside world looks like now... And it's funny, he's never mentioned it either... Of course even with all the drones and satellite imaging they have done I'm not sure even Dad and his coworkers truly know what to expect.

There are a couple other people in the auditorium as I pass through. Some coming back from the restrooms, a few just sitting along the walls whispering to one another. They must not be able to sleep either. I make my way to the door labeled "Authorized Personnel Only" and knock softly. The door opens a crack and a gruff, tired looking man stares back at me through the opening.

"Hey Stan." I smile warmly and he frowns at me before grunting out,

"James. She's here again." He backs away from the door and my father rushes over.

"Sam? Is it morning already? Happy birthday sweetheart..."

"Oh uh, no... Not morning yet. Still a few hours till my birthday too..." I grimace at the thought. I spent my entire teen years trapped in this bunker. Most girls would have gotten a sweet sixteen and a first car and first love by now... I got shots and minor radiation poisoning. Fun.

"Oh, okay... why are you up then? Did you need something?" Dad glances back over his shoulder as if he has something important to check on.

"No, I just... I had another nightmare and I just wanted to know what time we are getting out of here in the morning..." I shuffle my feet, realizing maybe i disturbed him for a dumb reason.

"Um... Whenever everyone's up and ready I suppose. We are still working out the details baby so I really ought to... Another nightmare you say?" He suddenly looks concerned and as if he's studying me.

"Uh, yeah, but it's nothing... I mean it was nothing..." I can sense my face beginning to flush.

"It was about that boy again wasn't it?" Dads face softens and he lets out a deep sigh.

"It's okay dad... I'm over it... I just can't get the memory to stop coming back while I'm asleep. I'll be fine. I should get back to bed..." I point back over my shoulder at the door to the living quarters. Dad looks like he wants to say something but instead just nods and shuts the door. I sigh. I don't know what I'd hoped to accomplish by seeing him but I don't think it went the way I'd hoped. Oh well, back to bed then. In just a few hours I'll be turning 18 years old, a legal adult, (if we even have laws anymore) and I'll finally be getting out of this hole in the ground that I've been forced to stay in for the last half a decade.

Chapter Five

"Happy birthday honey." Mom kisses me on the head as I sit on the edge of my bunk bed pulling on my shoes.

"You know, for the first time in the last 5 years... it is mom." I bound up off the bed and mom gives me a sad but hopeful look. I know she feels bad that I haven't had a normal life in a long time. Of course, it's not her fault but she still hurts for me. I suddenly feel bad for saying it like that and add, "I'm just super excited for Immersion day."

She smiles with understanding and glances behind me at something. I turn around to find a blonde headed little boy with a huge smile dashing towards me.

"Happy birthday Sammy!" Matthew recently lost his front left tooth and his grin is just the cutest thing. He's nearly seven now and boy is he getting big. He calls my mom Aunt Mary. We basically adopted them as family so he's kinda like my little cousin. Sara is always saying that he really looks up to me. I think it's so sweet. "Thanks buddy! Are you excited to go outside today?"

"Yep, my mom said I'm gonna get to see the sky!" He points up at the ceiling excitedly. I laugh and give him a nod of confirmation.

Suddenly a voice comes over the loudspeaker.

"Attention residents, Immersion Day will begin momentarily. If you wish to participate and leave the facility we ask that you make your way to the main lobby and form a line, if at all possible, in front of the exit doors now. Instructions will be given in the lobby before the doors are opened. Thank you."

Sara walks up and grabs Matthew's hand. She informs him that he has to stay with her the whole time. Mom steps up beside me and puts her arm around me, giving me a small squeeze. We all make our way together to the main auditorium.

The room is already filling up and we take our place in the makeshift line. Everyone is buzzing with anticipation and the volume in the room rises higher and higher. This is like a new holiday or something... probably closer to one than anything we do anymore actually. We haven't really celebrated any holidays in years. Not like we used to anyway. We don't have much to exchange for gifts at Christmas and there isn't any candy or flowers for Halloween or Valentine's Day. The only holiday we still make something of is Easter. We actually just did Easter about a week ago. And really that just means putting all the tables in the cafeteria together and eating dinner family style. Easter is supposed to be about new life and new hope. We haven't really felt like celebrating life for a while now. But today's different. Today there actually is a chance at a new life. It's almost like the hope that has died inside us has been resurrected today. We finally get to come out of this metaphorical tomb and start a new life. And it's clear I'm not the only one feeling it.

I look all around trying to spot dad. Finally I lock eyes on him. He's standing in the front corner of the room with other NASA employees. They pretty much always wear their uniforms so everyone can recognize them. They are kind of in charge. We don't really have a government down here but everyone looks to them for leadership since they know more... and they really accepted that role...

They bring out an old step ladder and dad climbs to the top. One of the others hands him up a bullhorn and he starts calling for everyone's attention.

"Alright everyone if I can have your attention. We are getting ready to open the doors. There's just a few things we need to go over though... First off, we need to stay together. If you want to wander a little further away from the bunker then please take a group of 3 or more. Do not go anywhere alone. We do not know what to expect as far as wildlife and we do not want to risk any unexpected um... issues... Secondly, the chambers will remain our base for the time being so we suggest returning here by dark each day. Next, atmospheric conditions have changed so the air pressure and gravity have been thrown off a bit. We've been allowing the air through the filters slowly over these past few years to allow everyone's bodies to adjust but if you do feel winded or nauseous please return to the bunker for medical attention and observation. Also if you find any food such as fruit or vegetables please don't eat it before bringing it back here to have it tested. Radiation could have mutated the plants and vegetation so we need to be sure it's genetically safe for consumption before ingesting. Um, other than that... just be cautious and alert and we will see how this goes."

Dad steps down off the ladder and he and Stan push through to the front of the line. From my place in the crowd I watch as the door to the corridor opens and a small stream of light glows through. Cheers of joy go up as the crowd begins to surge forward. It's almost like I'm in a mosh pit at a concert or something. I guess this is as close to that as I'll ever get again.

When we finally make it to the stairway Mom grabs my hand to keep me close. Sara and Matthew follow close behind. Matthew's little hand grips the back of my shirt so he doesn't lose me in the crowd. We stumble up the stairs, being surged forward by the anxious, shoving, people behind us.

We finally burst through the upper doorway and emerge into the outside world.

The NASA center seems to have been destroyed and lies in ruins around us. Either lack of maintenance or the elements have caused it to decay and deteriorate. Only pieces of the foundation are still in place over our heads. The sun shines so brightly through the beams overhead that many have to shield their eyes. I don't remember the sun being this bright... but maybe it's just because I don't remember a whole lot about the outside world period.

I look around and take in the scene. All around are scrap metal and rotted wood, all covered in vines and leafy weeds. The air seems to smell of ash and smoke and the heat from the sun seems more intense than it used to, like a weight is sitting on my head. I feel heavier in a way. Dad did say things had changed in the atmosphere and that the gravity and atmospheric pressure would be different...

"Wow... look Sammy... the sky!"

I snap out of my trance as Matthew tugs vigorously on my shirt tail. I turn and smile at him, ruffling his hair.

"I see it buddy..."

Not many people seem to be wandering off. It looks like everyone is going to be staying pretty close and just take in the scene for a while. I don't blame them... but I'm anxious to go exploring. "Mom! Let's go explore!" I spin around and hop excitedly in front of her with a pleading look.

She doesn't look as enthusiastic...

"Honey I don't think that's a good idea just yet... It may not be safe. I think we should stay close to base for the time being until everyone is used to the surroundings here."

"But mom! What's there to get used to here? Weeds and scrap metal? I want to go check things out!"

She sighs and shakes her head apologetically, "I'm sorry honey but you have to stay with the group and I don't see anyone else eager to explore today. Maybe tomorrow."

"I wanna explore!" Matthew says excitedly.

I give a small nervous grin in mom's direction and receive an angry glare in return.

"No Matthew, we are staying here with Aunt Mary for now." Sara jumps in adamantly.

"Aww man..." Matthew whines and his mother gives him a stern look. He instantly hushes and looks at me with a sad face.

I frown and sigh. "It's okay bud. They're right. It's probably not safe yet. We will go some other time."

Matthew agrees sullenly and follows his mom back inside the bunker.

I turn back to mom and she raises an eyebrow as if to ask if I meant what I said.

"I understand it's not safe for a child but in case you forgot I'm a legal adult today. I feel like I should have the right to come and go as I please." I fold my arms and huff.

Mom's face goes stern again.

"You may be 18 today but I am still your mother. And a New World may mean new rules, young lady. I would rather you be safe than get your way. So if you would kindly head back to the chambers we can get a bite to eat and revisit this discussion later." Her face seems to dare me to challenge her again... I don't. I'm angry, but I don't. I turn around and drag my feet back into the staircase, orange faced with silent frustration.

This is so not fair.

Chapter Six

People seem afraid to venture out away from base. I'm sitting up on a large rock overlooking the area. It's day 2 post immersion and I haven't been able to convince a group to go explore with me yet. I've asked everyone I've come into contact with and they all tell me they aren't ready to leave base just yet.

I watch as people build campfires, move debris around, and separate things they find into piles. Mom and Sara are sitting together by one small flame talking. Matthew has what appears to be a stick and is pretending to sword fight the air. I sigh and cup my hands around my face. My gaze drifts past the wreckage and down the street (well if you can still call it a street) towards a wooded area at the end.

The trees tower high, overlooking all of the overgrowth and debris before them. Eventually we are going to have to venture out. Who knows what could be out there? Am I really the only person out of the 100 something people that live in the bunker that has any sense of adventure left?

All of a sudden a hand plops down on my shoulder and I let out a scream. My body jerks instinctively away and sends me tumbling off the boulder I was on. I hit the ground with thud sending dust floating up around me. I groan as my body sends signals alerting me that my landing was not beneficial. Yeah brain, I'm aware.

"Oh gosh, Sam are you alright?" Dad asks as he steps in front of me holding out his hand. "I didn't mean to scare you..."

He's grinning and I can tell he's trying hard not to laugh.

"I just didn't expect anyone to come up behind me is all..." I say grabbing his hand and pulling myself up to my feet.

"Are you okay?" He asks again.

"Yeah, just a bruised butt bone probably." I start brushing the dirt off my rear end and my dad lets out a small chuckle.

"No Sam, not your butt. I was asking if you are okay in general. You looked upset when I came over." He smiles warmly.

"Oh, well in that case then no. Not really." He raises an eyebrow as if instructing me to continue so I go on, "I'm ready to get out there and explore! We've been in that bunker for 5 years and we are finally out and I'm ready to go see the new world out there dad!"

He frowns and lets out a deep sigh. "Sam..."

"See there you go again. Shutting me down before I even make my case. That's all y'all ever do." I cross my arms defiantly.

His face changes to one of anger. "Samantha Rose Overton! Now wait a minute. Your mother and I are just trying to protect you and everyone else in this camp. We have absolutely no idea what is out there. Mutated plants and animals, chemicals and pollutants, hazards created by the radiation and natural disasters. There is no telling what you might encounter and without weapons or tools or even adequate clothing. Absolutely no one is trying to hold you back or shut you down but we also understand the danger of going out there alone. Even in a group you could be at risk! We are all going to have to be precautious and take this one day at a time.

Wisdom child, it's called wisdom!"

The heat rising to my face. It's interesting how now we can see people's emotions much more easily than before due to the change in skin color. I'm sure my face is bright orange by now... "Well we are going to have to go eventually! When do you expect our food to run out, huh dad? Isn't that why y'all were pushing for Immersion Day? It was, wasn't it? You realized our food and water supply weren't going to last much longer and our only hope was to re-enter the world above to find supplies! Am I wrong?!"

I suddenly realize I've been yelling and by the look on dad's face he realizes it too. His face has lost all color. He looks scared to move. And I instantly regret my words when I see why. Glancing around us I notice that everyone has stopped talking and cleaning up. They are now all staring at us in dismay.

"Is that true?" Someone yells out from nearby.

Dad looks at me slowly and my stomach churns as if I'm going to puke.

"Dad I... I didn't mean..."

He turns and walks away without a word and everyone swarms after him yelling and crying and panicking. He doesn't answer anyone directly but just keeps telling everyone to meet him in the bunker and he will address them. Mom is nearby and she's glaring at me angrily. I duck my head and look away from her glare but I can still feel it digging into my skin.

When I finally get the courage to look back up, she's following the crowd into the bunker for dad's announcement. I begrudgingly follow. I'm one of the last ones in and the crowd is going nuts.

Everyone is freaking out and yelling over one another.

Dad is standing up on the step ladder again. He's yelling for everyone to get quiet and not having much luck. The other NASA guys are standing off to the side of the room shaking their heads. One of them catches sight of me and gives me a dirty look. I shrink back up the staircase a bit and sit down about halfway up sullenly.

Dad begins to explain as best he can over the crowd that, basically, yes it's true. He starts trying to relay their plan for finding food and supplies but the crowd is practically in hysterics by now. I suddenly get an idea and I glance back behind me up the stairs. The door is still open and light is flooding in. Everyone is focused on dad and the food shortage so nobody is even looking in my direction anymore...

I stand up as quietly as I can and back up slowly out of the staircase. As soon as I'm out I glance around to make sure no one is still out here to see me. The land around me is empty. Nobody in sight. I glance back with slight hesitation but I push past it. With the tree line down the street clearly set in my vision...

I take off running.

Chapter Seven

My feet thud heavily over the dirt and cracked pavement as I race towards the wood line. I don't bother looking back but keep my eyes fixed on the grove of trees before me. I leap over debris and obstacles as I go, glad for the little bit of extra height in my jumps from my body's adaptations.

When I reach the trees I stop at the edge. I'm tempted to turn around and look back but what if they are outside now... what if they are looking for me and seeing them makes me change my mind?

No. I can't risk chickening out.

So I push through the vines and brush into the woods. There doesn't seem to be a clearing as far back as my eyes can see. It's all trees and vines and bushes everywhere. The leaves of the tree's seem a brighter green than I remember. Everything seems brighter than I remember to be honest. Maybe that's from the radiation or maybe it's just my memory failing.

I decide to walk straight back as much as I can. Of course circling a tree in my way here and there... but this way I figure I can avoid getting lost. When I'm ready to go back I'll simply turn around and go straight back the way I came. Simple right?

So far I've seen no animals. No birds or rabbits or squirrels... nothing living. Aside from the plants and trees... A cool breeze rustles through the trees above me but otherwise it's eerily quiet. I'm shuffling on when something suddenly stabs me in the leg. I squeal and look down to find a thorn vine wrapped around my leg.

A small stream of blood is already dribbling down to my ankle.

I bend down to pull the vine loose. Carefully unwrapping it from around my leg so as not to cut myself more. Examining the cut on my leg I decide it's actually pretty deep. It's definitely going to need treatment.

"Great... just great. Like we have the extra medication back at camp to be doctoring my stupidity..." I mutter to myself, beating myself up for not watching where I was walking better.

Something nearby hits the ground with a loud "thwack" and startles me so much I fall over. Forgetting all about my leg I bolt up off the ground and spin around, looking for the source of the sound. There's a tree limb and I assume it must have fallen out of a tree nearby. Of course, I don't know for sure because I obviously wasn't paying close attention to my surroundings to begin with... so who knows if it was already there before or not. But seeing nothing else that could have caused it I decide to blame the limb.

I continue walking on for a bit before I notice a rotting log up ahead of me a ways. Curiosity gets the best of me and I head over to it. It's covered in moss and rot and looks frail. I give it a good kick and the area I kick falls apart inwardly. After the dust settles insects of all kinds can be made out inside.

"Huh, so SOMETHING survived anyway." I announce to myself.

Everything in the log, ants and beetles and centipedes and worms, all seemed to have mutated slightly. Some are bigger than they used to be, some different colors, and some seem faster than I remember. I guess everything that survived was changed by the impact. Of course, I'm not sure much else survived at this point... I'm guessing the only reason these guys survived is because they did what we did and hid underground.

"Smart little bugs aren't you?" I say, not the least bit concerned that I'm talking to worms...

I step over the log and look around. Something nearby catches my attention. A little ways to my right I notice a bush with some kind of colorful berry on it. I start to walk over but hesitate. It's off my straight path... But I can just come back over to the rotted log and then head back from there right? I decide I can and continue to go ahead and check it out.

When I reach the bush I realize it's a lot bigger than I had originally thought. It looks about 4 feet high probably. I'm 5 foot 6 and it goes up to my elbow. The berries on it look like blueberries but instead of a dark navy blue color they are a bright royal blue. I decide to grab a handful and stuff them down in my shorts pockets. Maybe when I head back I can have dad test them. If they are edible maybe it can help our food supply.

I walk around the bush collecting the plumpest berries I can find. When I come around to the back of the bush, there is a sudden rustling nearby. I freeze.

'What if it's a mutated bear or something?' I think to myself. The sweat beads are already forming on my forehead from fear.

I slowly turn my head around and see... nothing. I look back and forth in all directions but there's nothing as far as I can tell. Slowly I begin to tiptoe back around the bush. I know I'm not crazy. I heard something... something is out there.

The rotted log is just up ahead and I start making my way back to it. Glancing over my shoulder every so often to make sure there's nothing there. When I reach the log the sound comes back again. I spin around in every direction. Nothing.

Now I'm freaked out. So I take off running. I run as hard and as fast as I can back in the direction of camp. My feet move beneath me so swiftly almost like I'm flying. I'm not, of course. But at the rate I'm moving it certainly must be what flying feels like. The blood on my leg has dried some but the stress I'm putting on my legs right now reopens the wound. I grimace at the sting of the wind against the cut.

I still have a weird sense that something is following me. But I keep glancing back and seeing nothing. Soon the edge of the trees can be seen and I leap towards it, landing just before the clearing. I stop. The camp is just down the street. I haven't been gone long and I'm not sure if anyone has even noticed yet or not.

I turn back to look one last time into the forest. And this time I catch sight of something. Ever so briefly... it was only a split second... but it was there. I gasp and back up out of the woods in disbelief. For a moment I stand there staring at the woods in shock. It can't have been and yet, I know what I saw. For just a brief second I caught sight of it before it disappeared behind a tree...

It was an arm. A human arm.

And it was lime green.

Not yellow...

Green.

Chapter Eight

As I get closer to the base I can hear my name being called. I cringe. I'm going to be in so much trouble... Dad isn't going to want to see me, nonetheless talk to me... But I have to tell him about this... And have him test these blueberries too, of course. I slip my hand in my pocket and make sure the berries are still there. They are.

I can't stop thinking about that arm. That means someone survived up here. It means we aren't alone. What if there's more than just one? What if...

"SAMANTHA ROSE!!!" Mom's voice is clearly upset. It sounds like a mix between anger and fear. Up ahead, she's standing at the camp and we lock eyes. Her face is orange. I duck my head as I get closer. I decide not to even stop unless she demands it. I just head straight for the bunker. She watches silently, tapping her foot as she glares at me.

My shoulders drop lower as I pass her and she follows behind me, still not saying a word. Once we are inside she clears her throat and I grimace as I slowly pivot to face her.

"Well," she starts calmly, "go ahead and explain yourself then."

"I... uh... I don't really know what to say. I'm sorry I caused everyone to panic. I'm sorry I disappointed you. I'm sorry I had to sneak off without warning... but I'm not sorry for going to explore."

She looks like she's starting to get angry again but somehow keeps her cool.

"You could have been killed." Even as she says it she notices the cut on my leg. Her eyes evaluate it and then look up at mine as if to say I told you so.

"I'm fine. It's just a little cut."

"Little? You need to go to the triage station and get that looked at. You're lucky it wasn't more than a cut. Do you have any idea what you could have run into?" She runs her fingers through her carrot colored hair. Thin gray hairs have slowly been appearing the last few years and her age is starting to show through. She's tired. And it's not my intention to add to her stress. But I can't just be locked up in here forever.

"I found something." I say it very matter of factly but as her eyebrows raise I suddenly rethink my decision to tell her about the arm...

"What? An animal?" She looks concerned and hopeful at the same time.

"Um... I uh..." I suddenly remember the berries and reach into my pocket and pull out a few, holding them out for her to see. "I found berries."

She looks at them and then back at me worriedly, "you didn't eat any of those did you?"

I sigh with relief. "No, I knew better. I brought them back for dad and them to test."

"Good. He's in the APO room. He's still pretty upset with you.

Make sure to apologize to him when you take those berries to him.

Everyone is scared now so he's under extra pressure and stress." She gives me a look that seems to scream 'it's your fault' and I inwardly groan.

"I really didn't mean for that to happen..." I mutter again...

"I'm sure you didn't. Maybe it'll serve as a lesson that you should be slow to speak next time?" She raises an eyebrow at me.

I nod and she pats me gently on the cheek before walking away. I head to find dad. Dreading the conversation that might ensue.

The door to the APO room is shut and keypad locked as usual. I knock and sigh, running my fingers through my hair nervously. The door cracks open and a middle aged woman with blonde hair pulled back in a bun and dressed in NASA get up glares out at me. She doesn't look thrilled to see me.

I have seen her around but I don't know her name. You would think after 5 years I'd know everyone. But this lady is really reserved. I think being the only female NASA personnel that survived must have been hard for her. She probably feels like she has to prove herself. She also appears to be as angry with me, as my dad probably is...

"James... Your daughter is here." The woman huffs and shuts the door in my face.

Um... okay...

The door reopens slowly and my dad slips through the crack. He looks tired and stressed. Which is probably my fault too. I look down at the floor. I can't even bear to look him in the eye.

"Samantha." His voice is calm but there is a slight touch of anger in it.

"Hey dad..." I whisper.

"I'm glad to see you survived your rebellious little adventure." He sighs, now his tone just sounds more disappointed than anything. I honestly think that's worse...

"I... I'm sorry for running off but I had to see what was out there... And I didn't figure anyone would even notice after the problems I caused... which is another thing I'm sorry for..." I look up at him with sincerity.

With a deep sigh his shoulders sag a bit. As if he's releasing some tension and letting down his guard. I take it as a good sign.

"Look Sam, everything we've been doing, the rules we've made, they are all for the good of the group. We are trying to protect everyone. I'm trying to protect you. And your mother. It's not our intention to keep you or anyone else locked up. But we have to be cautious. We don't know what's out there yet." His eyes scan my face as if looking for the slightest sign of understanding.

"Or who..." I mutter. I say it so softly it's barely audible.

"What was that?" Dad asks. He seems to perk up a bit and I wish I hadn't said it. I backtrack hard.

"Some food!" I quickly answer, "There's uh, food. I found some berries." I pull the vibrant blue berries from my pocket and hold them out to him.

"Sam! Here let me see those!" He holds his hand out and I pour the berries into his hand. He picks one up and holds it up in the light to look at it more closely.

"I uh, didn't eat any so don't worry. I figured I'd bring them back here to have you test them or whatever first." I'm extremely relieved he seems to have forgotten my little slip of tongue earlier.

"This is magnificent! Of course we will have to test them first but... were there more?!" His excited tone makes me feel like I'd redeemed myself.

"Yeah a whole bush. About 4 feet tall. I could take you if you want!" I say eagerly.

He shakes his head and pats my shoulder. "Not yet but we will test these and see. Thank you Sam." He starts to open the door and head back in again but stops and turns back to me, "was there anything else?"

The surprise probably registered on my face and I shook my head violently. "No! I mean, not that I can think of... I just, I wanted to apologize and get you those um... berries. That was it..." I try to relax a little hoping my reaction didn't give anything away. He studies my face for a moment before nodding.

"Apology accepted. Love you honey." Pulling the door open he slips back inside. Just before it shuts behind him I shout back,

"Love you too dad."

Chapter Nine

"Where's uncle James?" Matthew's small voice echoes from beside me.

I glance over at him as I lay on my bottom bunk. He's on the bunk next to me with his head hanging off upside down and his feet swaying through the air. His long blonde hair hanging off the bed looks so funny I can't help but grin.

"I'd imagine he's testing the blueberries I found today." I say before looking back up at the metal bars above my head.

"How long does that take?" He moans impatiently and I laugh.

"I don't know bud. They have to make sure they are safe to eat."

"I know but it's been like forever already!" He groans and rolls over before climbing back up to sit criss cross applesauce on his bed. I sit up too and shake my head in amusement.

"Yeah, I know. But they have to use a lot of high tech equipment and stuff and it takes a while."

"Why don't they just make a faster machine? Like one that can just scan it and be like boop beep boop and done. Then like spit out a paper that says 'safe to eat'?" He makes little poking motions like on an invisible keyboard as he says it.

I can't help but laugh and lean forward to ruffle his hair. "Maybe you should suggest that to them sometime." I grin as I stand up and stretch my arms over my head. Then I notice the double doors opening and dad shuffling through them. "In fact, here comes your chance now."

Matthew spins around on the bed and shouts anxiously as he scuffles his way off the bed and rushes towards my dad. "Uncle James! Uncle James! Can we eat the blueberries?! Huh can we? Can we?"

He's spinning circles around dads legs and dad pats him on the head.

"Well we don't have enough of them yet Matthew."

The excitement begins to build up in me. "So they are edible!?" My voice probably sounds just as giddy as Matthew's does. Dad nods.

"Yes!" I shout and fist pump the air.

"We need to send out a team to pick as many as possible and to also bring back some snippets from the roots so we can replant them here. Would you be able to draw a map to them?"

My smile drops instantly. "A map? What? No! I mean... I'm going with them!"

"Samantha I don't think it's safe to..." I cut him off.

"Safe? I'm the one who went out there and found them in the first place and I am fine! I deserve to be on that team!" My face is burning with heat.

"You went against a direct order and could have been killed!"

"But I wasn't! Nothing..." I pause remembering the arm, "Nothing happened to me and I'm not drawing a map. I go or they can find it on their own, eventually." I stomp my foot and instantly feel foolish, like a toddler throwing a temper tantrum. But I hold my face and don't let it show.

Dad sighs and waves his hand. "Fine. Whatever. I'll assemble a team and yall can head out in the morning. Get some sleep and be ready. Or I just might go with that second option." He stomps off and I relax my face, slightly relieved and slightly embarrassed.

Turning back towards our beds I suddenly realize Matthew had been watching the whole exchange. His eyes are wide but he doesn't make a sound. I cringe.

"Bedtime bud. Our moms will be in any minute." I say softly and he nods and jumps in bed. I sigh and climb in mine too.

Morning seems to come in the blink of an eye and it becomes apparent that someone is shaking me. My eyes squint open and Matthew is there, leaning over me.

"Sammy... Sammy you have to get up... They are going to leave without you if you don't..." his soft whispers resonate in my ears and I bolt up, smacking my head on the metal bars above me. Matthew makes a face as if feeling my pain but knows better than to ask if I'm okay.

"Oh..." I moan and rub my forehead as I slide off my bed and grab a pair of shorts and a t-shirt out of my cubby. I race to the bathroom and see my dad and a group of about 5 others by the front door talking. Dad notices me and makes eye contact. He looks annoyed and I give him a "I'm hurrying" look as I rush through the bathroom door.

I'm out in under two minutes ready to go. The team is already up the stairs and outside. I bolt out the stairway hatch and the sun nearly blinds me. Using my hand as a shield above my eyes I spot the group and rush over.

"I'm here, I'm ready!" I announce as I take my place next to dad by the others. Some of them give me a look that seems to suggest they don't necessarily appreciate my being there. Dad being one of them.

"Alright. You all know what you need to do. Just get as many of the berries as possible as well as some of the plant and roots." He hands each of us a plastic grocery store bag as he says it. "If you happen to come across any animals do not engage them." He looks right at me as if he thinks I'm the most likely to try to grab a wild radioactive animal in the woods. Okay, well, I can't really blame him for that but I don't intend to be messing with any wildlife today other than blueberries.

We all agree and head out. When we get to the edge of the woods I notice how nervous most of the others look. There's a younger guy who's maybe in his 20s and an older guy maybe mid 40s. Then there's me and two other women who are both a few years older than me. I don't know them very well but the oldest is about 26 and she has a very bossy personality. A real take charge type. The other girl is more shy and doesn't talk much. The older guy doesn't talk a whole lot either but not because he's shy. He more or less has a 'you're not worth my time' attitude. The other guy is tall and chipper but also somewhat shaky and tense.

From what I gather the bossy girl's name is Megan, the shy girl is called Ella, the tall guy is Andy, and the older guy is Mike. Megan seems eager to go in but I think it's just her desire to be in charge. "Alright let's get a move on!" She sounds off.

I step forward and wave my hand.
"Sure, follow me."

"And just who put you in charge?" She hisses at me and steps up so close, her hot breath on my face.

"Um," I say, stepping back a bit, "I'm the only one who's been out here before and I know the way to the berry bush. Remember?"

"Yeah, so show us the way but don't think for a second that means you're in charge. You're just an immature kid who thinks she can break the rules for a little fun when she's bored. Let someone more mature call the shots." She huffs and holds her arm out as if to tell me to lead on.

Mike lets out a small chuckle from the back of the group and Megan shoots an evil look at him but says nothing. He's obviously laughing at the idea of Megan and her 26 year old self claiming to be mature.

I grin in his direction and he rolls his eyes. Apparently he wasn't defending me with his laugh but rather finding the both of us beneath him. Megan whistles as if to get my attention like one would a dog. I grit my teeth and stomp past her. Twigs crinkle on the ground beneath us as the others follow behind me. The heat from Megan's eyes glares into the back of my head as I walk along. I want to turn around and see but I don't want to give her the satisfaction. I've barely spoken to this girl in the whole five years we've been trapped underground together and after just 5 minutes she's become my rival.

We push through the brush and vines into the forest and head straight, as I did before. Nobody talks and the woods are silent aside from the sound of our footsteps and breathing. We've been walking a good ways when Megan breaks the silence.

"Are you sure you know where you're going?" She moans and I let out an exasperated sigh. I suddenly can't wait to be back at the bunker. She has actually managed to make me miss that place, something I didn't think possible, after only a short time spent with her.

In the distance I spot the rotted log and point towards it. "The bush isn't far from that rotten log okay. Chill."

She makes a face and crosses her arms defiantly.

"Do you know how many rotting logs are probably in this forest? How do you know that's even the right log?"

I roll my eyes and rub my temple. I suddenly have a slight headache. Wonder where that could have come from... "I just do. So come on." "Whatever." She sighs.

We reach the log and I start looking around for the berry bush that I remember was within sight of it.

"Hey! There are bugs in this log!" Andy shouts excitedly. I turn to find Andy and Ella knelt down next to the log, examining it. Mike is watching and looks interested too but when he sees me looking he scowls and looks away.

"Yeah, I noticed that when I was here last time." I smile proudly.

Megan rolls her eyes, "We are supposed to be looking for berries. Not worms." She gives me a dirty look as if I'm the reason for the delay. I glare back and point behind her.

"The bush is right over there okay? What's it going to hurt for them to explore a bit?" I challenge.

She looks me in the eye and says nothing for a solid ten seconds before waving for the others to follow her. Mike doesn't hesitate to fall in step behind her. The other two look at each other and then apologetically at me before chasing after them. I shake my head and follow.

Everyone starts filling their plastic bags and Megan announces that she will collect the vine and root samples, sighting her experience with botany in college before the asteroid hit. Nobody responds to her and she takes that as collective permission.

I could care less about who gets the sample. I'm mindlessly picking berries off the bush as I scan the land nearby, wondering if the person I saw before is still out there. Are they nearby? Are they watching us? What other things/people are out there?

A hand suddenly appears in front of my face, waving frantically. I snap back to the present to find a frustrated Megan waving in my face.

"What?" I ask, annoyed.

"Quit daydreaming and let's head back. We got all we can for now." She points at the bare bush and turns to head back towards the log. Suddenly she lets out a blood curdling scream and drops her bag of berries on the ground, spilling a good bit. I rush over to her and look around but see nothing.

"What was it? A spider?" Mike chuckles from behind us as Andy and Ella bend down to pick up her loose berries.

Megan's face is now nearly cream colored as she slowly lifts her arms to point at the tree above. We all look up and follow her finger. There's nothing there.

"Thh... there... it... a... person." She stutters to get her words out and when she does the others all three look at each other and then laugh. The color returns to her face almost instantly and she stomps angrily.

"There was a person! I saw them! They were green!" She insists angrily. The others laugh harder, I stay silent.

Mike interrupts the laughter, "Nobody at camp has green skin. The darkest one is Sid who held the door open till the last minute during the impact for stragglers and even he ain't darker than a lemon. You saw the wind blowing the leaves or something. Now come on and let's get back." He shakes his head, still smiling in amusement.

"I know what I saw!" She insists and now the others stop laughing and just roll their eyes and march past her. Her gaze turns to me and she narrows her eyes.

"You didn't laugh." Her voice is accusatory rather than thankful and it makes me frown, waiting for what I'm sure is coming next. "You believe me don't you? You've seen it too! I bet you saw it when you were out here before!"

Now the others turn around and give me a surprised and interested look.

"Let's just get back to base okay?" I mutter as I start to move past her. But she doesn't let me. She puts her arm out to stop me and steps in front of me.

"That wasn't a no. You did see it." Her eyes grow wide and so do the others behind her. I groan.

"Fine. Okay. Yes I saw someone. Happy now? Can we get out of here already?" I push her hand away and stomp past the other three whose jaws are all agape.

Nobody says a word the rest of the way back but I notice they all walk a little closer to me and everyone keeps looking around anxiously. Even Mike doesn't look comfortable anymore. And

Megan just glares at me angrily as if I've done something wrong.

Maybe I have... maybe I should have warned them about the arm. I don't know. But I do know I'll have no choice but to come clean about my secret now. Because the first thing Megan's going to do is tell dad. And I don't even blame her.

Chapter Ten

We march back to base in silence. Megan looks steaming mad and keeps her eyes ahead while the others keep looking around concerned. Probably making sure whoever is out there isn't following us... We get back and head straight to the APO room to drop off the berries with my dad.

Mike knocks and dad opens the door.

"Oh good! You made it back okay. Let's take the berries to the garden." He waves for us to follow him and heads off. The others all look at me.

Mike raises an eyebrow at me as if to ask when I plan to tell dad about the person. I make eye contact with Megan and instantly regret it. Her look is asking the same question but in a more threatening way. I get the feeling if I don't tell dad, she sure will. Andy and Ella look down at the floor when I look their way.

"I will" I mouth to Mike and Megan as we follow dad. Megan lets out an unbelieving snort from behind me and I grimace but refuse to turn around. I follow dad into the garden area. There's a table set up near the garden and some ladies are already waiting when we arrive.

"Alright y'all, just leave all the bags up here and these lovely ladies will get the vine planted and the berries put away in the freezers." He points to the table and starts to walk back out. Megan clears her throat and I shoot her a look.

"I'm going okay!" I growl in her direction and she shrugs and turns back to the table.

I run my fingers nervously through my hair before calling after dad, "Dad, hang on." He stops and turns back to me, looking a little confused, "I uh, can we talk a minute? Like privately?" I glance back at the others who are all staring. They suddenly turn back to the table and pretend to be busy.

"Of course." He looks a bit concerned now and motions to the door, letting me go first. I lead him up and out of the bunker. Not many are outside right now it seems; so I find a quiet spot near some fallen slabs of concrete and sit on one. Dad stays standing in front of me.

"What's going on Samantha?" His eyes narrow and I gulp.

"Um, well, I didn't exactly tell you everything about what I found in the woods before..."

"What do you mean you didn't tell me everything you found? What else did you find exactly? An animal?" He looks both annoyed and concerned as he questions me.

"Sort of... technically I guess..." I'm not doing well at this.

"What kind of animal? Was it mutated or something?" He pulls out a notebook and pen from his back pocket and looks excited. I groan.

"Um, what kind? Well, uh... Homosapian?" I try to give a small laugh like it's no big deal but dad doesn't look amused. He slowly lowers his pad and pen and looks me straight in the eye.

"You saw a person?" His voice is calm but stern. I guess I expected him to be more surprised. Maybe he doesn't believe me? "Yeah... a green one. Not yellow like us. And... Megan saw it, I mean... them... today too." I study his face as I say it. He remains unmoved. Now I'm really confused.

"And you're sure it was nobody from the bunker?"

"Green? Do you know anyone in the bunker that turned green? Like lime green dad. It... they were lime green." I reaffirm.

His hand lifts to his chin as if he's thinking and he turns around to sit down next to me. I look at him in shock. How can he be this calm and collected unless...

"Wait... you knew didn't you?!?" I stand up and face him.

His eyes when he looks up at me tell me all I need to know. It's true. He did know. I stand there, mouth open, speechless.

"Yes and no Sam. I knew there was a slight possibility that there might be at least one person still alive but I didn't know for sure if they made it or not." Noticing my face becoming even more confused he sighs and pats the concrete next to him again. I narrow my eyes but finally sit and face him as he begins to explain.

"About a year after the impact when we finished the vaccine and everyone here was vaccinated, we started sending up drones to record data and give us an idea of what the upper world had become. Well... the very first drone we sent out recorded a video that shocked us all. About a mile or so down the street, or so we figured based on the spotty footage we were able to salvage, the

drone had come across a human being."

My eyes get wide but he moves on before I can say anything, "A teenage girl from what we could tell. She was not in good condition due to the excessive radiation and the new atmospheric changes. Her body couldn't fight through it and adjust quick enough and it was obvious she wouldn't make it much longer. But of course, the risk of someone going out there after only having just been vaccinated was too great..."

I interject angrily at this point, "So you just left her to die out there?!" My mouth is agape and my stomach twists into knots. Dad looks at me surprised.

"Of course not! Well, I mean we couldn't go get her but we didn't do nothing! We sent the drone back out with all the vials of vaccine we had left. It was only 3 or 4 unfortunately. But it was the best we could do. The drone delivered it to her along with a note instructing her how to inject it and explaining what it was. We didn't figure she would understand the science behind it but we hoped she could use it nonetheless. But in her condition we were afraid it may have been too late. The drone did return without the vials though and the next time we sent it out there was no sign of her." He looks sad but at the same time thoughtful.

"So... you think the person we saw in the woods could have been her? Like maybe the vaccine worked and slowed the process just enough for her body to adapt in time?" I ask and he nods.

"It's possible... In fact if you did see someone it is really the only explanation that makes sense..." a soft, relieved, smile forms on his lips.

I leap up excitedly and begin pacing back and forth anxiously.

"Well we have to go find her! No wonder she was following us in the woods! She was probably just as surprised to see people as we were to see her! Can you imagine being alone for five years! Having to survive without anyone?"

Dad shakes his head. A cool breeze drifts through and blows my hair into my face, tickling my nose. I brush it back behind my ear. Dad stands up and pats my shoulder.

"We have no idea where she lives in the woods, Sam. We don't even know how far the woods stretch or even if this girl is still in her right mind. For all we know she could have some severe mental instability and could be dangerous. We should proceed with caution..."

He scratches his chin and looks thoughtfully up at the sky. The sun is starting to set and vibrant pinks, purples, and blues fill the atmosphere.

"We can't just leave her out there though..." I mutter.

Dad looks back down at me and sighs, shaking his head again. "No, we can't. And we won't. But we will have to be careful. And we can't look tonight. We will assemble a group tomorrow. Right now we should be getting back in. It's time for supper."

I realize this is the best I'm going to get out of him and I agree, following him into the bunker.

Chapter Eleven

I moan as the speaker system screeches on overhead waking me up from a deep sleep. The voice on the com comes through rough and scratchy.

"Residents, there will be a mandatory meeting in the auditorium before breakfast. Again this is not optional. The meeting will begin in 10 minutes. Please make your way to the auditorium in an orderly manner. Thank you."

I growl and shove my pillow over my head. Suddenly someone snatches it off me and smacks me upside the head with it.

"What the!?!" I bolt up banging the back of my head against the bars of the bunk above mine... again. I grimace and clutch the back of my head, rubbing it gently as I twist around to face whoever assaulted me with my pillow. I'm not sure whether to be surprised or not when I find Megan glaring back at me, arms crossed with my pillow still clutched in her right hand.

"What's your problem?" I ask her as I toss my legs over the side of my bed and rub my head again.

"They said there was a mandatory meeting. Thought maybe you didn't hear them since you were under this." She throws the pillow at me and I catch it right before it hits my face. "Thought I'd help you out." She flips her hair and smirks as she saunters off.

I leap up and grab my hair brush and start combing through my tangled mess of a head as I chase after her. When I get to the auditorium it appears everyone is already there. Megan is standing towards the back and she glances over her shoulder, giving me a dirty look as she sees me running up.

I stop next to her and put my brush in my back pocket before quickly pulling my hair up into a ponytail holder. Megan watches me for a moment with an eyebrow raised in judgment. When I give her a 'what are you looking at?' face she simply rolls her eyes and turns back away.

I'm tempted to say something to her but suddenly, my dad's voice rings out and I turn to see what's going on. As usual when they make announcements, dad is up at the front of the crowd standing on a step ladder. I'm beginning to wonder why he's always the one who does the announcing. Do the other NASA team members just not like public speaking or does dad volunteer or what?

Dad begins explaining to everyone what he told me yesterday, as well as what I told him. Upon hearing that there is another human being alive out there the crowd became to whir. Everyone started whispering and mumbling among themselves and with everyone doing it soon it became a loud rumble.

Dad manages to get everyone quiet enough to continue but every-one seems distracted after that.

"So we need a volunteer team to organize a search party. This search party will be looking for the girl but also looking for any animals or food or supplies that might possibly still be out there."

The rumble starts again. People start yelling out questions and demanding answers. Dad looks tired and frustrated but he does his best to answer each one. But after a few minutes he suddenly steps down from the chair and the female NASA employee climbs up it with the bull horn.

"That's enough questions. If you want to volunteer stay in here and we will give you the information and get started. If not, find somewhere else to be!" She snaps at the crowd and everyone quiets down a bit and starts to disperse.

Before long the room that was just full of people is now down to a group of around 25. Megan and myself included. I'm not really surprised she'd want to go. She obviously has control issues. Of course she wants to be the one responsible for finding her.

The NASA woman motions for us to all gather around her closer and once we do she starts talking, no bull horn this time.

"Alright. Head count shows there are 23 of you that stayed. So with me that's 24. We will divide everyone into groups of 4 and each group will be given a list of things to look for and a backpack. Everyone's backpack has a first aid kit and a can of mace."

I raise my hand and Megan gives a snort. The NASA lady huffs in my direction.

"What Overton?"

"Well, first off, you can call me Sam if you want. Secondly, I realize I don't know your name. And third, mace? Really?"

She looks annoyed. "First off, I'd rather not. Secondly, my name is Kate but you can just call me ma'am. And third, yes mace. Unless you would rather risk getting attacked and maimed by some mutated beast?" She scowls.

"You think mace is going to stop a mutated animal if we come across one?" I raise an eyebrow. She glares at me and turns back to the group as a whole.

"When, if, you find anything food related please bring a sample back to the lab. You will have a small shovel in your pack as well as zip lock bags to put samples in so as to prevent cross contamination if necessary. Here are your packs and your lists." She motions behind her where dad is coming out of the APO room carrying arm loads of backpacks.

Kate starts handing out papers to each of us as dad hands us each a bag.

"Once you have your bag and list, get in groups of four." She says as she makes her way down the line of us.

As she passes, the rest of the group starts separating. Megan and I are at the end of the line and by the time we get our papers we look around to see that pretty much all of the groups have formed. Megan shoots me a disgusted look and sighs. Someone taps me on the shoulder and I turn around to see Andy.

"Guess we are going back out together again then?" He rubs the back of his neck before nodding over at Megan.

"Yeah I guess. Who's going to be our fourth though?" I glance around the room and see all the separate groups each discussing their list. A couple of the groups start pulling their backs on and heading out.

"I am." The voice comes from behind me, Kate striding over with her back pack already on her back. "Let's get a move on."

She stomps past us and waves her hands, gesturing for us to fall in behind her. We all grab our bags and race after her. Megan rushes up and plants herself directly at Kate's side. They start talking about the plan while Andy and I follow a few feet back.

Andy starts trying to make conversation but as we enter the edge of the forest I become too distracted to listen. He's going on and on and occasionally gives a nervous chuckle. I watch the tree tops looking for any sign of the girl. Every once in a while I'll nod or mutter "uh huh" as Andy talks but I really have no idea what he's talking about.

A sound above makes me stop in my tracks. I scan every branch of the trees above me. Suddenly something grabs my shoulder and I jump a bit and let out a small yelp.

"Um, sorry? I was just asking how old you are..." Andy looks very apologetic as I turn to face him. I sigh and shake my head.

"I'm sorry Andy. I just really wanna find this girl... I'm 18 now. And you?" I ask but glance back up above again. The sun shines through the treetops sporadically.

"I'm 21. But I've been told I look a lot older than I am..." he lets out a small nervous laugh which draws my attention back again.

He really does look older than 21. His brown hair is slicked back cleanly and he's so tall for his age he basically towers over me. He's very clean shaven but his facial features are quite firm. His square chin is probably what gives him the more mature appearance. This is the first time I've really taken a hard look at him. And I'm surprised to find he's actually kind of cute.

I suddenly snap back to reality and shake the thought from my head. A relationship is the last thing I need to be thinking about at this point in time.

"Wow, yeah you definitely look older than that. I never would have guessed. Umm, maybe we should ask Kate if she has a specific game plan or something..." I'm sorry for ending the conversation but I really want to focus on the mission and I have the feeling he could easily become a distraction if I don't nip this in the bud here.

He looks disappointed but nods.

"Hey, uh, Kate?" I holler out and speed up to catch up with her and Megan.

A growl comes from her direction as she turns to face me.

"Thought I told you to call me ma'am? What is it Overton?" She and Megan both give me the same annoyed look.

Great... there's two of them. Just one is twice the other's age.

"I just wanted to know what the plan is exactly. Are we just blindly walking through the forest or what?" I gesture largely to our surroundings.

"Each group that entered the tree line was to head in a different direction. I let each group know which direction they should take before we left the bunker."

I frown, "I don't remember that..."

"Well, I figured since I was in your group I didn't need to tell you which way to go because I could just show you. Are you satisfied now?" She crosses her arms as if challenging me to question her authority. I don't. But I'm not happy about it.

We continue on. I'm beginning to notice most of the woods look exactly the same. There doesn't seem to be a whole lot of variation or distinct markers anywhere. Just dirt and leaves and trees as far as the eye can see in any direction.

"Look!" Megan shouts and we all jerk our heads around in the direction she points.

"What!" I yell excitedly, scanning the scene, "is it the girl?!"

Megan looks confused for a minute then shakes her head, "No. It's food. Over there, that tree."

We follow her and as we get closer I realize what she's referring to. A tree comes into sight that's covered in a blue and red spike covered fruit.

Megan looks proud of herself as she turns to us, wiggling her head in a 'haha I found it first' tease. I raise an eyebrow at her and stifle a laugh.

"Congrats. You found a prickly pear tree. Now how do you expect us to collect it? Did you want to be the one to grab it since you found it? By all means!" I wave my hand in the direction of the nearest fruit and watch as her face drops. Andy giggles behind me and I try to hide the blush rising into my cheeks.

Kate gives me a look as if to call me immature and proceeds to circle the plant. She and Megan start discussing ideas and Andy intersects with an idea of his own. The three continue talking and arguing over different methods. Out of the corner of my eye I sense movement and I quickly turn to investigate.

It came from somewhere on my right but there isn't anything abnormal. I glance back to make sure the others aren't paying attention and then slip away. Listening carefully as I tiptoe from tree to tree. A sound comes from up ahead. Leaves crunching. The sound gets further and further away and I realize whatever it is must be running away. I take off. Without even a thought I dart after the sound, dodging trees and leaping over fallen limbs.

After a few minutes of running it's there, ahead of me. A squirrel.

You have got to be kidding me. I chased a squirrel?

I'm gasping for air as I slide down against a nearby pine. 'Well', I think as I gasp and try to catch my breath, 'at least now we know some animals survived besides just insects.'

I watch the squirrel as it climbs a nearby tree and starts cleaning itself. It's absolutely huge. The biggest squirrel I've ever seen. It's like the size of a really fat rabbit. And what's weirder still is it's solid black. I mean, I knew squirrels came in different colors and all but I've never seen an all black one before. At least, I don't remember ever seeing a black one... dark gray maybe...

Suddenly the squirrel goes still. Its ears perk up and it starts looking around. Then out of nowhere it just falls from the tree and hits the ground with a thud. I gasp and leap up, running over to it. I'm slow to approach it, scared it might still be alive and attack me. But as I get closer I can tell it's no longer breathing. Tears start to form and I blink them back. What is wrong with me? I didn't kill it... and now I can take it back to the bunker and they can study it and see if it's safe to eat...

I crouch down and start to reach for its tail when a voice behind me shouts, "don't touch it!"

I scream and fall backwards, my butt landing hard on a rock or something. I moan and roll onto my side, rubbing my sore behind without shame. Someone nearby lets out a small snort. Amused by my pain no doubt.

"It's so not funny!" I sit up and turn my head, expecting to find Megan, Kate, and Andy. What I find instead is a pair of bright green, hairy legs. I gulp as my head follows the legs up.

Above me stands a boy about my age. He's dressed in basketball shorts and a tank top. His abs show through his shirt and I blush a little. He has strong cheekbones and a firm chin that's adorned in a fine, dark goatee. His dark brown hair hangs just above his eyes and swings towards the left. He flashes me a grin and holds a hand out.

I nervously take it and let him help pull me up. My mouth is draped open but I can't bring myself to close it. He looks amused and steps past me. I turn and watch as he pulls a cloth and a plastic bag out of his shorts pocket. He drops the cloth on the dead squirrel and then lifts it and tosses it in the bag. Then he glances back at me, and noting the confused look on my face, explains.

"I shot it with a poison pin. It's not safe to touch it till it's been cleaned." He ties the bag in a knot and wraps the handle around his wrist.

"Oh..." I say it as if I know what he's talking about. I can tell by the look he gives me that he's called my bluff.

"Well, are you going back to your posse now or did you wanna come with me Sam?" He tosses his head to the side a bit to sling his hair out of his face and looks at me curiously.

"I uh..." I suddenly realize something and narrow my eyes at him, "Wait! How did you know my name is Sam? I never told you my name..." I cross my arms and watch him suspiciously.

He chuckles and flashes that dazzling smile again, "Well, for one I've seen you in the woods several times and I've heard your friends calling you."

My shoulders relax some as I realize that it must have been him I saw that first day and that Megan saw the next. That would explain it. But he doesn't stop there.

"And secondly, how could I ever forget my best friend?" He shrugs like what he's just said isn't a big deal.

"Your best friend? But I don't..."

"Even know me? Well not since before the asteroid hit anyway. Sucks we never got to finish that social studies project huh?" He winks at me.

Realization hits and I gasp.

"Sh... Shane?" I look him up and down again in shock, trying to put my memories of him up against this new, grown up, (green) version.

"Finally got ya speechless huh Sam?" He shakes his head and turns to walk away.

After collecting my thoughts I dash off after him. Pulling up beside him I grab his shoulder and sling him around, embracing him. He stiffens.

"Uh, Sam I don't..." he starts to object to my hug but stops when he realizes I'm suddenly sobbing into his chest.

He pats my back uncomfortably and I can sense the tension in his body as I hold him. When I finally regain composure I pull back, wiping my eyes dry with my arm. He looks at me a little bewildered and runs some fingers through his hair.

"Sorry..." I mutter, "I just... I thought you were dead. All these years I thought you were dead." My voice cracks a bit but I manage to avoid bursting into tears again.

Shane sighs, "Yeah, well I thought the same about you. Or at least I knew it was likely... Until I saw you in the woods the other day. And I thought it was you so I followed but it was kinda hard to tell since you're older and... you know, yellow. But then I heard your friends saying your name that next time and knew it was you." He shrugs.

"They aren't really my friends... and you don't exactly look like you used to either. You're... green... How did that happen anyway? And how did you survive? And what about the girl my dad sent the vaccine out to? Is she alive? Do you know her?" I realize my voice is rising with each question and tell myself I need to calm down.

Shane raises an eyebrow at me and gets a thoughtful look on his face, as if he's mulling over my questions. The woods around us are eerily silent. The mid-day sun shines through the tree tops casting shadows around us on the fallen leaves and twigs. Finally Shane responds.

"So the vaccine came from your dad then?" I nod and he says, "I think maybe you should go first. Tell me everything that happened on your end since the alarms went off."

"I feel like this conversation may take a while..." I moan.

He looks around then points up at a thick, low hanging limb on a tree nearby. "I've got time." He leaps up and grabs the limb, lifting himself up and letting his feet dangle off the edge. A grin forms on his face as he pats the space next to him, "ya coming up or what?"

Chapter Twelve

We've been in the tree for an hour as I've been telling him all about what happened from my end. I told him all that I could remember from the day of the event up until I met him in the woods today. He stayed pretty quiet the whole time. Like he was thinking over every word I said carefully. Sometimes I'd pause to get his reaction but he'd just nod and wait for me to continue.

"So uh, that's what happened... We didn't think anyone else could have survived... until yesterday when dad told us about having sent the vaccine out to that girl..." I explain and he nods.

"Cassie."

"What?" I ask, confused.

"Her name is Cassie. She's alive and well by the way. And she's the reason I, and everyone else, are alive too. Well, part of the reason." He stretches his arms over his head and groans. We've been sitting here too long apparently.

"Everyone else?" I give him a surprised look, "more people survived? How many? How?" I bounce excitedly and the tree branch shakes slightly. I get still, concerned the branch might not be able to handle too much excitement.

"Settle down a bit and I'll tell you." He lets out a small chuckle. Then he sighs and starts in. "When the sirens went off and everyone went into panic mode my parents woke me up and we ran. We had no idea where to go. My parents tried calling yours but the tower was down and calls wouldn't go through. Then we heard some people on the street saying they were opening up the storm shelter at Houston University. So we headed there. The science professors on campus had some protective gear and resources that helped shield us some. It wasn't enough to last forever though. After about a year we were all so sick. Really everyone was on their deathbed. They didn't expect us to live another month. The radiation was just too much and we just didn't have enough protection. Cassie and a few others volunteered to go look for help. To see if anyone else survived and could help us. When she came back with the handful of vaccines we were all amazed. She had taken one already and brought the rest to us. And she already looked so much better. Still sick and green but not deathly ill anymore. The chemistry professor, Dr. Carter Smith, took the vials and managed to replicate the vaccine. She made enough for the whole company. Sadly we lost a lot who were already too far gone though..."

He hangs his head and his voice gets low. A breeze blows through, shaking the leaves above us and causing me to shiver. I'm not sure if it's just the wind or if the words he spoke were partly to blame too. He looks really hurt. I want to comfort him somehow but I'm not sure what to say...

"I'm so sorry..." I lay a hand on his arm and he turns to face me. He studies my face and nods before continuing.

"Anyway, a lot of us survived though and made a home for ourselves in the campus dorms. We've been there since. Dr. Carter kind of became a leader to us after saving us like she did. There were about 60 of us who survived. But a few have had children since then. Seems newborns don't need the vaccine because they inherit the immunity from their mothers." He shrugs as he finishes his story. Then he hops down off the limb and looks back up holding an arm up as if to ask if I need help getting down.

I shake my head and hop off the limb. I land hard and grimace a bit. He gives me an amused smile but says nothing.

"So y'all were able to reproduce the vaccine and make more of it? That's great! It's so awesome to know other people survived! All these years I had no idea... we had no idea. I just can't believe we aren't alone! That others survived! That you... survived. I missed you..." I look back up at him fondly.

"Yeah, I missed you too Sam." He smiles softly. Suddenly he jerks his head around.

"What is..." I start but he shushes me. Holding a finger up to my mouth. I freeze, fearing some wild animal must be coming or something. But then I hear it.

"Samantha!"

"Sam!?"

"Overton! Answer us right now!" I groan and Shane raises an eyebrow.

"I need to go." He mutters.

"What? Why? Don't go!" I object.

"Sam, look, I'll see you again okay. But I need to go. I need to get this squirrel back to camp and... I just don't think it's time for everyone to meet up just yet. I had to talk to you. But I think we should discuss what we've learned with our individual groups before getting too involved..." He runs his fingers through his hair again.

"But why?" I question. I can hear the others getting closer and it's apparent that Shane does too. He looks nervous.

"Look Sam, you just have to trust me. I'll meet you here again tomorrow. Okay?"

"Okay... I guess..." I make an annoyed face.

"Bye Sam." He nods behind me and I turn to look. In the distance, Andy, Megan, and Kate are yelling for me as they walk. I turn back around and Shane's gone. I shake my head.

"I'm over here. I'm fine!" I yell to the others as I turn back to head over to them.

The color of the light shining through the treetops is starting to change and I reckon it's getting close to supper time. The thudding of my team's footsteps on the leaves and twigs coming towards me causes me to shift my wait nervously. The sound makes my heart quicken and dread, as if I'm being chased, rises up in me. I take a few deep breaths as they approach and slow. I'm not sure what I'm going to tell them yet.

"Where the heck did you go?!" Megan demands angrily as they stop before me. Her right hand on her hip and her eyebrows raised in a 'how dare you' scowl.

"Why did you run off?" Andy asks, concerned. His voice is soft and curious as if he truly believes I wouldn't have without good reason. Some of the tension in my shoulders eases when I look into his eyes and see grace.

Unfortunately it comes right back with Kate's question that follows...

"What is wrong with you?" She hisses at me and sticks her face right up in mine menacingly. I'm tempted to step back away from her but, as caught off guard by the question as I am, I manage to stand my ground and respond calmly.

"Look I didn't mean to worry you or anything but I saw something and went looking for it and ran into..." I pause letting my voice drift a moment as I thought back to seeing Shane again for the first time.

Heat rises to my face and apparently my sudden change in color confuses Kate. She steps back and tilts her head a bit, as if trying to understand my reaction.

"Ran into what? A tree?" Megan is already working her face into a grin at the thought. Apparently she assumed my blushing means I'm embarrassed. And now I am with that thought...

"No!" I snap at her. "I did not run into a tree." I cross my arms and roll my eyes. She flips her hair, amused that she got a rise out of me.

"Then what did you run into Overton?" Kate narrows her eyes at me suspiciously.

"I uh... well there was a squirrel..."

Megan starts to laugh but Kate shushes her promptly. Her face twists into one of surprise and disgust but she goes silent.

"You actually found an animal?" Andy chimes in, stepping towards me excitedly.

I nod. "Yeah, it was huge though. And black instead of brown or gray... but I uh, think they must be edible..."

Kate looks interested as she questions me, "and how exactly do you know that?"

I rub the back of my neck nervously. Shane didn't say not to tell about him... in fact, if I remember right, he said we should tell our people that others survived.

"I found more than the squirrel..." I watch Kate's eyes narrow and Andy's open wider in surprise and curiosity. Megan tries to act disinterested but I can tell it's a front. "I saw a person..."

"The girl?!" Andy's face is lit up as he asks hopefully. But he cocks his head in confusion when I shake my head no.

Megan rolls her eyes. "Probably someone from one of the other search groups." She huffs and waves her hand around in a mocking circle.

"It was a boy. He was green. I... I knew him... before..."

Even Megan whips her head around at that. They all stare at me in shock.

"Did you speak with him?" Kate finally manages to regain composure and ask.

"Yes. For a while. He killed the squirrel and..." I glance around and notice it's getting pretty dark. "Don't you think we should head back?"

"Don't you think you should tell us what he said?!" Megan snaps at me in response but Kate holds up a hand.

"No, she's right. We need to get back. She can tell us ALL back at base."

She turns and starts off in the direction they came from and we all reluctantly fall in behind her.

A few other groups are at the edge of the woods and we wait for the last group to arrive behind us before all of us head back to camp together. Megan begins whispering with someone from another group and I notice them glancing over at me as we walk. Murmurs begin to spread throughout the group and eyes keep looking in my direction. There's warmth in my cheeks again.

We head down the stairs into base and dad greets us.

"Well, any luck?" He asks. The entire group goes silent and turns to stare at me. Dad cocks his head to the side confused and looks to me for an explanation.

I rub the back of my head nervously.

"You could maybe say that..."

Chapter Thirteen

They've been in the room for a while now. Dad and the other members of NASA haven't come out of the APO room in over an hour. They were all pretty shocked when I told them about Shane. I don't think they ever expected the vaccine to actually help those who are outside the bunker. They thought the chances of it working for that girl were minimal and they definitely didn't expect her to be able to find someone who could clone it.

After I told them everything Shane told me the other members of NASA had nodded towards the room and my dad looked reluctant to follow but did. I have no idea what they're even talking about. I'm sitting out in the main room leaned against the wall to the left of the APO room. I was hoping I'd be able to hear through the wall but no luck. The only noise that gets through is the sound of whirring machines and the occasional beep of a computer.

I look up to see my mom coming across the room towards me.

She's carrying a plate. Apparently, I missed dinner. I sort of expect her to scold me for it but she doesn't. She hands it to me and I thank her. Then she slides down the wall to sit next to me.

Her face looks very solemn and I set the plate down next to me and turn to her.

"What's wrong mom?" I ask softly.

She sighs and looks up at the ceiling. Her eyes start to water in the corners but she blinks it away.

"I have a confession to make..."

The tremble in her voice causes my stomach to knot up.

"What?" I ask nervously.

"The night the asteroid hit... when we were in the car heading here... You were freaking out because you couldn't get a hold of Shane... and

I told you not to worry because I had warned them the night before to come here if something happened..."

I try to think back to that night but it's mostly all a blur now. But I do remember worrying about Shane.

"Yeah..." I mutter, pretending I remember the scene.

"Well... I... it's just that... I..." a tear trails down her cheek now and she doesn't bother to wipe it away. "Sam... I lied."

"What?" My heart nearly stops beating in my chest as I try to process what I'm hearing.

"I never called Mrs. Baker or warned them the night before... It was confidential information... We weren't allowed to tell anyone in case it didn't happen. But you were so upset and scared and in order to calm you down... I... I lied."

She's full on crying now and puts her head in her hands. I suddenly get a flashback image in my head. I remember being in the car that night now. I remember mentioning my fear for Shane and Mom telling me that it was okay and that she had called them... And I remember Dad's face when she said it. He had glanced at her so confused and she had given him a look back as if to say 'be quiet'.

It all makes sense now.

My temperature rises in anger. I want to understand why she did it. I want to be okay with what she's telling me. I can tell from her face how much she regrets it and I want to forgive her... but I don't know that I can at the moment. The implications here, what could have happened, it's inexcusable.

So I rise to my feet and head to the bed chambers without looking at her or saying anything at all. She doesn't try to stop me. Her sobs linger in my ears as I leave her there.

Time seems to fly by as we all wait for the "council" (which is what we've started calling the NASA members) to decide what they want to do with the information Shane gave me. My stomach growls and I clutch at it with a moan. Matthews blond head appears over the edge of the bed as if on cue.

"Didn't you eat dinner?" He giggles.

I sigh and shake my head. "No, mom brought me a plate but... no I didn't eat."

"I ate dinner... but they never give me enough! My stomach is bigger than they think it is! So I'm always still hungry." He makes a dramatic gesture to show just how hungry he is.

This time I'm the one giggling. This kid always knows how to cheer me up.

"Well, we can't have that. I think we'd both better go find a late night snack. What do you think?" I roll off the bed and hold out my hand.

His face lights up and he grabs my hand, immediately pulling me in the direction of the door. We make our way to the cafeteria. I notice I haven't seen mom around since our talk earlier. I wonder where she's gone...

In the cafeteria we find Sara sweeping up. She glances up at us and raises a slightly disapproving eyebrow. Matthew steps behind me and whispers to me that he doesn't think his mom wants him eating this late. Placing her broom against a wall nearby Sara saunters over.

"Hello Samantha. I believe there's a plate for you in the oven. Your mother said you may come back for it later." She nods in the direction of the kitchen and then turns her eyes to Matthew. "I suggest y'all hurry and eat. It's almost bedtime."

She then turns and leaves the room. Matthew dances excitedly at having gotten permission to get a snack.

We head into the kitchen and I pull my food out from the oven. It's cold now but I don't want to take the time to reheat it, so I eat it cold. I find Matthew some fruit to snack on and we start to head back to the bed chambers. But as I push the door open to head back out of the cafeteria it hits someone.

My dad pushes his arm through the opening and slips in.

"I'm sorry I hit you with the door..." I mutter. "Did y'all come to a decision?"

I noticed Matthew looking from me to my Dad confused. Sara must not have told him what's going on yet. So I kneel down and instruct him to go back to bed and I'd be there soon. He nods and runs off.

We watch to make sure he's officially gone before Dad turns back around and answers me.

"Well, it was a close vote... But I think we've decided that making contact with them is the right thing to do."

"That's great!" I shout and dad gives me a look as if telling me to calm myself. I try to settle down.

"You will have to try to find Shane again and set something up."

"Okay! I will! I can go tomorrow to look for him and we..." I'm not finished with my thought before Dad interrupts me.

"Listen Sam, when I say it was a close vote... I mean I was the tie-breaker. Half of the members of NASA think it's a bad idea. If this goes south I don't think we can convince them to continue trying... Keep that in mind and be prepared."

I try to process what I'm hearing. Why would they think it's a bad idea to meet up with people we haven't seen in 5 years? People we loved and thought we lost? How could that possibly be a bad thing?

Dad can tell the wheels in my head are turning and he shakes his. "Look Sam, I can't go into details. But they have their reasons... I just want you to be careful about how you go about this. We may only get one shot to make this reuniting thing work..."

He pats me on the back and tells me to head back to bed.

Tomorrow could be a long day and I'll need to be rested and ready.

I begrudgingly accept and head back.

Making my way up towards my bed I notice mom on hers. She appears to be fast asleep but I don't know how she could be since she obviously hasn't been there long. It's more likely she's just pretending so that I don't try to talk to her. I sigh and head over to my own bed.

"Night Sammy!" Matthew whispers down at me from his bunk.

"Night bud. Get some sleep." I smile up at him and he yawns and rolls back over.

I lay on my back staring up at the metal above me. Why didn't the council members want to find the people above? What reasoning could they possibly have? Will I be able to find Shane tomorrow? Who else survived that I might know?

So many questions running through my mind, but I finally roll over and try to shut my brain down and rest.

Chapter Fourteen

It's like six in the morning. Way too early in my opinion for gallivanting through the woods. But dad insisted I find Shane as soon as possible, so apparently, that means rising with the sun. Honestly though I'm so excited to see him again myself that I don't really complain.

Dad and I are marching towards the edge of the woods when footsteps thud up behind us. Dad signals for me to wait. Kate bounds up next to us in cargo shorts and a NASA tee with a backpack hanging off her shoulder.

"Um, what are you doing here?" I question. She raises an eyebrow at me as if I'm supposed to know the answer to that already. Then she glances at my dad who sighs and responds for her.

"I told Kate she could go with you." He already looks pained, preparing for my inevitable resistance.

"Why? I don't need a babysitter!" I gesture wildly in frustration.

Dad rolls his eyes. "She's not going with you to 'babysit' you. It's just not safe for anyone to travel alone when we don't know what's out there."

"Shane is out there. People, loved ones we thought we lost, are out there!" I exclaim.

Dad looks me dead in the eye and nods. "Yeah, people who by all scientific explanation shouldn't exist and may have... changed..." "Changed?" I look from him to Kate and then laugh in annoyance and disbelief, "have we not changed too? I don't remember growing up yellow dad."

His lips tighten and he looks like he wants to say something but then decides against it.

"Let's get a move on Samantha. I'm going with you and that's that. Let's stop wasting time arguing and head out." Kate stomps past me towards the woods. I start to protest again but dad shoots me a look and I begrudgingly turn to follow after Kate.

We make our way back towards the area where I met Shane last time. Once we pass the bush they harvested the prickly pears from I decide to start calling for Shane.

"Shane! Shane, are you here?!" I yell, hands cupped around my face.

Kate jerks her head around to face me and shoves a finger to her lips before scolding me.

"Are you crazy?!" She hisses.

"Well, how else do you expect us to find him?" I place my hands on my hips and make a face at her.

"Didn't you say he told you where they stay?"

"Well... yeah... but I mean everything looks so different now and I was so young last time..." I frown and glance around me, "I mean, even this forest wasn't here back then was it? I have no idea how to get to Houston University."

Kate raises an eyebrow and pulls a map out of her bag.

"I don't think that map is going to be accurate anymore Kate." I announce. She ignores me and begins studying it anyway.

I watch her curiously until she finally folds it up, puts it away, and points.

"That direction." She says, pointing off to our left.

"If you say so. I still don't see why it's such a big deal for me to call for him. What do you think will hear me? Another giant squirrel?" I giggle and she gets that really annoyed scowl again and steps closer to me. Honestly a little too close for comfort, so I can't help but back up a foot.

At this point I'm almost a little scared to look her in the eye.

"Did your friend happen to say how many of them there are?"

The question surprises me and I tip my head back up to look at her again. I don't know what I was expecting to come out of her mouth but that wasn't it. I shake my head slowly... a lie.

"I don't... I don't think so. Or at least... If he did I don't remember. Why?"

"Have you ever thought about the fact that your dad and all the other members of NASA, myself included, were able to get all of their families to safety, but nobody else?" Her eyes actually widen a bit as if she's thinking about it herself for the first time. I start to say something but she continues and I shut my lips again. "Looking back now I'm realizing that maybe we didn't quite go about it the way we should have..."

She almost looks pained at this point and I can't help feeling a twinge of empathy for her.

"I mean, yeah, that was... look I'm mad about it okay? I told my mom... I said some things to her that I..." I stammer over my words, trying to hold back the tears as I realize the pain now in Kate's eyes is the same pain I saw in my mom... Right before I stopped speaking to her.

"That anger you're feeling," Kate sighs, "My guess is they're feeling it too."

At first I'm confused as I try to process what she just said but it doesn't take long before reality hits.

"Wait... so you think... You think they might actually, like, hate us?" A cool breeze blows and a few small leaves fall around us. Kate nods and turns away from me to start walking again. I follow behind, still trying to process the implications of what she's just suggested.

"So when we get there... What exactly did you have in mind then? I mean you don't think they would try to, like, hurt us or anything do you? Because I really don't think Shane would ever..." I trail off. Kate doesn't bother turning around. She simply keeps moving forward, but does at least offer a response after a moment of silence from me.

"Look, I have no idea what to expect. I just didn't like the idea of you going alone. Just in case. And I'm sure your friend would nev..." She doesn't get a chance to finish when suddenly there's a cracking sound nearby and we freeze. She holds up her hand as if to tell me to stop, like she actually had to do that... I turned into a statue the moment the sound hit my ears.

Both of our heads twist around looking for the source. My eyes tip up above watching the tree line. Suddenly they spot something... or rather, someone.

"Kate..." I whisper softly. She glances over at me and I nod my head up towards the person in the trees. Kate follows my gaze and lets out a small gasp. Overhead there's a girl crouched on and limb shortly ahead of us. Her skin is lime green and almost seems to sparkle in the sunlight that's shining through the trees above. Her blonde hair appears braided over her right shoulder.

She's watching us silently. And while her gaze doesn't appear hostile it also doesn't necessarily give off a friendly vibe either. We all just sit that way for several minutes, staring at each other. Finally I decide to make the first move.

I step a foot in her direction and smile up at her. "Um, hello! I'm Sam! Do you know Shane?" I give a small wave and glance back at Kate. A decision I immediately regret as she's glaring at me as if I'm an idiot. My shoulders shrink as I turn back around.

The girl in the trees narrows her eyes at me and tilts her head ever so slightly in a somewhat distrusting, yet curious, manner. Then she nods in the direction of the wood line ahead, as if to tell us to follow her, before bounding off through the treetops.

My first instinct is to dart after her but as I try a force grabs hold of my shirt collar and yanks me back so hard I almost fall on my butt for the second time.

"What the heck are you doing?" Kate growls and I huff back at her as I shake her off.

"We don't have time for this! Come on!" This time I speed off after the girl before Kate has a chance to re-grab me. She lets out an exhale of frustration behind me but her footsteps soon fall in behind mine.

As the girl bounces through the trees above us some small twigs and leaves fall in her wake. She seems a little faster than us and I have a hard time keeping her in my sights. But it doesn't take long before we reach the end of the woods and she leaps out of the tree onto the busted concrete ahead. I stop just before the opening and Kate bounds up beside me. She bumps me with her hip and I almost lose my balance. Apparently she's angry at me for my decision. Oh well. At this point, I'm pretty sure she's never going to not be angry with me.

The girl looks around and then nods in the direction of what appears to be a run down city ahead. I start to walk that way but Kate hisses at me yet again. A deep sigh escapes my lips and I turn back to face her again.

"What is your deal?" I huff.

"We don't know if we can trust her. You shouldn't just be blindly following her. We don't even know who she is!" Kate gestures behind me in the direction of the girl. But her eyes suddenly get wide and she drops her hand quickly, looking down in a somewhat guilty manner. I slowly turn around to find the girl standing directly behind us, head cocked sideways and one hand on her hip. It's apparent she heard every word.

"Hello," I start, holding my hand out to her for a shake, "I'm Sam." She stares at my hand disinterested and nods. "I know. Shane told me. Plus you yelled it at me in the woods. Why do you think I directed you to follow me?"

"Well I... umm..."

"Your friend advised you against it. Why didn't you listen to her?" The girl looks curiously from me to Kate and I get a strange nervous feeling all of a sudden.

"Good question." Kate mutters but I notice her ever so subtly take a small step backwards.

"I just... Look, I don't know. Maybe I'm just more trusting than her. You said Shane told you about me? Do you know where he is?" Without even realizing it my hand moves up to rub the side of my face as I ask. My nerves are a little on end but I don't want to give that away to Kate now.

"Again," the girl rolls her eyes, "it's why I'm here. But..." she pauses thoughtfully and her gaze falls on Kate again, who clears her throat anxiously and looks away, "Your friend may be right to not be so trusting of everyone."

"What do you mean?" The question catches in my throat as I too take a small step back.

She raises an eyebrow at me, "Oh, I'll let Shane explain. But we should get going if you wanna see him today."

Dust floats up as she spins on her heel and darts off in the direction of the city. I give Kate a glance and her head shifts side to side ever so slightly as if to say she's considering it. But I decide there's no time to let her settle on a decision and I bolt off again.

Instead of frustration this time there is only a soft exhausted breath from behind me as her footsteps chase mine.

The girl stops running as she pulls up beside a brick building covered in vines. She slowly slides along the wall and peers out around the front of the building. I slide up behind her with Kate hot on my heels. I'm not sure what the girl is looking for but I don't ask. Finally she motions for us to follow her and we walk quietly in her tracks. There was a road through the town at some point but the concrete is full of potholes the size of cars now. You pretty much have to watch where you step the whole time you walk.

"So, what's your name?" I ask, trying to end the eerie silence.

"Shhh..." The girl scolds me. I zip my lip and glance back at Kate who gives me a smirk. Apparently she's amused that somebody other than her is telling me to shut up. I roll my eyes at her and turn back around.

The girl freezes. She looks around as if she's listening for something. Kate and I go still as well and twist our heads around, trying to pick up on what the girl hears. Voices in the distance seem to be getting closer.

"Crap... come on!" The girl hisses at us and rushes into a nearby building. Kate and I look at each other uneasily before chasing after her. When we get into the building, her footsteps sound on some stairs nearby. The stairs are covered in dust and cobwebs and the girls' footprints are left behind on each step. We race up after her, still unsure where she's leading us. Up flight after flight we go, finally making it to the top. The girl busts through the door to the roof and holds it open for us. We race through and look around. There's nothing up here.

"Let's go." The girl whispers as she takes off running past us.

"Go where exactly?!" Kate growls back.

The girl doesn't respond, but she doesn't have to. Because before we even have a chance to react she leaps off the edge of the building. Kate gasps and I race over to the edge to look. There's another building below and the girl is racing across it towards yet another.

"You have got to be kidding me..." Kate mutters under her breath. But before she can stop me I leap off the edge as well. Kate exclaims some not-so-nice words above me. I hit the roof of the next building hard and stumble a bit. Kate lands behind me with a thud but I don't look back. I simply get my bearings and then race after the girl again.

We go leaping from roof to roof and I'm having a blast. Kate on the other hand is extremely annoyed. After about 5 or 6 buildings the girl climbs down the side of the last one using the vines growing on it. We follow after her slowly, careful to tug on the vines first to make sure they're strong enough. Once our feet hit the ground she turns back to us.

"Over there." She says pointing towards what appears to be an old storm cellar. She heads over and opens the old doors exposing a set of rickety old stairs. I glance back at Kate who looks at me as if I've lost my mind.

"There is no way I'm going down there. And you shouldn't either if you had any sense. We don't even know this girl!" She glances at our guide almost apologetically, as if realizing that her statement was insulting and yet not backing down from it. The girl simply shrugs, affirming that she did not take offense to Kate's warning. "Well then fine... stay out here." I reply, turning to go down the stairs. The girl looks troubled by this and turns back to Kate.

"It would be best if you came with us. However, I understand your skepticism. If you wish to remain outside please stay out of sight... I'm not sure it's a good idea to let anyone see you right now... I'm sure you understand." The girl glances around nervously.

Kate narrows her eyes, "And why is that?"

"I would really prefer Shane explain. He's waiting for us down here. Again, if you refuse to come just stay out of sight and Sam can explain everything when she gets back."

Kate sighs heavily in frustration. "Fine. I'll come. But I do not like this one bit." She addresses me as she says it and I simply shrug and begin marching down the stairs. Kate insists on being the last one in and the girl instructs her to make sure she closes the door behind her. Kate gives her a suspicious look but does as she asks.

Chapter Fifteen

The stairs curve around the corner making them appear longer than they actually are. As soon as we round the corner, Shane appears up ahead. He's standing in what looks to be an old run down wine cellar. The walls are lined with wooden barrels connected to rusty taps. The lighting is dim but I can see Shane grinning from ear to ear. I race towards him and embrace him in a hug.

"Miss me that much?" He coos and warmth spreads across my cheeks. I pull away and give him a small shove.

"Shut up!"

He laughs and runs his fingers through his hair. His eyes shift behind me as the girl and Kate round the corner.

"Thanks Cassie." I follow Shane's gaze and notice the girl nod before plopping down in an old metal chair in the back corner.

"Cassie?" My eyes widen, "You mean, you're the girl that my dad sent the vaccine out to? You're the one who saved everyone?"

She looks hesitant at first but eventually nods, offering nothing more. Cassie stands back up and thumbs in the direction of the stairs. "I'm going to go back up and keep watch... Just in case..." She bounds up the stairs and out of sight before getting a response from any of us.

"In case of what?" I turn back to Shane curiously. "Cassie told us on the way over here that maybe I shouldn't be so trusting... What did she mean by that?"

Kate steps up beside me, "Yes, please do tell." She smirks as if she's just waiting to say 'Ha I told you so' at me.

A frown forms across Shane's face and he leans back against a barrel, rubbing his left temple.

"Look, I tried to talk to President Smith and the council about this and... they didn't take it very well..." He sees the look of concern on our faces and continues. "They made a rule that we're not supposed to talk to or interact with the underworlders in any way. Basically, Cassie and I are breaking the law by bringing you here.

And if we're seen with you it could be bad for us... and you."

I can't believe what I'm hearing. "What?! Why? We just want to help!"

"I know... but they don't care... they resent your kind for not warning people and saving them. They don't feel you can be trusted." He sighs.

"Our kind?! Underworlders? We're all human beings! How can they separate us like this? It's... this is so wrong..." Tears begin welling up in my eyes.

Kate has remained quiet so far, taking it all in. Finally she speaks. "Sam, I think we need to go."

"What? No! We have to do something about this. Maybe if we could just talk to that President Smith person? Explain to them what happened... That we never meant to... Well most of us didn't mean to... I mean..." At this point I just break down. I'm sobbing uncontrollably as I try to wrap my mind around this situation.

Kate looks uncomfortable and twists her head towards the staircase. "I'm going to head back out... I'll give you a minute to calm down. But we can't stay Sam. I'm sorry. We have to get back and let your dad know what's going on. Maybe he can come up with a plan to negotiate and reach out to them but there's nothing you and I can do." She slips back up the stairs quickly, leaving me and Shane alone.

Shane steps forward and wraps his arms around me. I melt into his chest, weeping. "Look... Sam... we'll figure it out. It'll be okay somehow. But for now it probably is best if you head home."

I look up at him and try to wipe my eyes dry, it doesn't work well. He watches my face, his deep red eyes sucking me in. There's a small bead of sweat making its way across his forehead. For the first time I noticed just how hot it is here. Or maybe it's not the temperature... What if it's something else... I decide to test the theory.

I slowly lean upwards and close my eyes. I have every intention of kissing him... but he suddenly moans and takes a step back. I open my eyes and notice he seems to be avoiding looking at me. He rubs the back of his neck nervously. Now I'm completely embarrassed.

"Sam I..." he starts to look back up at me but seeing the pain on my face he groans and looks away again.

"Oh... are you and Cassie?" I whisper, suddenly nauseated.

"What?" He whips his head back to face me again, "Cassie? Oh, no! She and I are just friends..."

I'm not sure whether this makes me feel better or worse...

"So what then? The law?" I duck my head and rub my arm. *'Maybe I should just leave...'* I think to myself, glancing back at the stairs.

"No." He says it very matter of factly, shaking his head slowly. "It's been a long time, Sam. And back then we were just friends... And you're upset right now, and rightfully so... but I just think maybe we should give it a little more time before we just jump headfirst into something..."

"Oh..." I'm not really sure what else to say. I guess he's probably right. Jumping head first into things is usually how I roll... And I guess I have to admit that it's also gotten me into my fair share of trouble... He's probably being really smart and mature about this. But it hurts...

He looks at me with this face that seems like longing mixed with pity. *'Great...'*

Shane reaches out and pushes some hair out of my face, tucking it behind my ear with a sad smile. "Sam... I'll see you again okay?" "Okay." I mutter, unsure how that can happen at this point.

"Cassie will show you back to the middle of the forest. And Sam... I know your friend up there seems to think some kind of peace negotiations can happen... But just... Be prepared okay?"

"Prepared for what?" That nervousness in my chest comes back again. The same one that I felt when Cassie first told me I shouldn't be so trusting.

"I don't know. I just get the feeling that it's not going to be as easy as your friend Kate thinks it will... the Overworlders council are strict and vengeful. And they are really mad at your dad and his co-workers... Y'all just be careful. And don't assume anything..."

"Okay..." I mutter as he hugs me one last time and ushers me up the stairs.

When I exit the wine cellar I find Kate and Cassie standing guard.

"Ready? We need to get back." Kate raises an eyebrow at me and I nod.

She falls in line behind Cassie and I follow at the back. We slip around buildings and duck behind trees and old cars and whatever we can until we make our way back to the woods. Cassie gets us back to where she found us and then nods as if to say goodbye before turning and running off.

Kate notices that I'm lagging a bit, "You alright Sam?"

I glance up at her and sigh. "Not really. But I guess it is what it is."

"We will figure something out..."

"Yeah..." I say before muttering softly under my breath, "We hope..."

She doesn't hear it as she turns back around, leading the way back to the bunker in silence.

Chapter Sixteen

"No one is to go in the woods again until we figure this out. Do you understand me?" My dad stares at me intensely, waiting for my response. I can tell by the tenseness in his shoulders he's expecting me to argue. I don't.

"Yes sir..." my head hangs low in acceptance. Dad's eyebrows furrow as if he doesn't believe me but he nods.

"Good. And Sam?" He lifts my chin gently. "We will do everything we can to make peace okay? I'm sorry... I truly am... we never wanted... I mean... you know." His hand drops and he turns away, heading back to the lab.

Kate stands in the doorway behind him, head low and one arm rubbing the other nervously. As my dad walks past her she glances back at me with sad eyes. Something tells me she doesn't have much hope for these negotiations. But then, she isn't a very optimistic person to begin with.

~~~~~

A few hours later all the members of NASA exit from the lab, my dad trailing behind them. Kate appears to be holding a small metal box of some kind as she marches for the exit.

"What's going on?" I stand up from against the wall I've been patiently waiting by. My dad looks at Kate, who nods and picks up her backpack from beside the corridor to the stairs, slipping it on silently.

"Someone has to go deliver the message... our request for peace... Kate is the only one who knows the way." He notices my face scrunch up and stops me before I can say anything, "She's the only mature adult who knows the way. She's going. Alone. Don't argue."

I let out a shriek of frustration and turn away. My dad doesn't bother trying to stop me as I head into the other room to my bed. Pushing
~~~~~

through the double doors I glance around. Some people are playing cards on the floor, others are talking on their bunks, and others appear to be napping. Everyone is trying to make themselves busy until dinner.

"Sammy! Over here!" I glance ahead again towards my bunk and find Matthew hanging over the edge. I race towards him and lift him back up.

"Matty you're gonna fall!" I put a hand on my hip and shake my head at him as he sits up straight again.

"Nuh uh. I'm spider man!" He shoves his wrist out at me in the "I love you" symbol.

"Right... of course you are. Wanna be a superhero huh?" I smile and climb up the ladder a bit to see him better.

"Yeah! Like Kate!" Matthew giggles.

"Kate?" My eyes narrow and I try to shake it off before he notices. Thankfully he doesn't.

"Yeah. Aunt Maryann says Kate is going to go to the people on the surface and make friends with them so we can help them! That's what heroes do... help people!" A rumble comes from his stomach and he giggles.

"Right..." I glance around the room again and notice Mom and Sara talking a little ways away. Mom glances over and makes eye contact with me. I give her a 'we need to talk' look and I can tell from the face she makes that she understands. I turned my attention back to Matthew, "Hey Matty, why don't you go ask Cook how much longer till supper?"

He nods and I hop down off the ladder to give him space to climb down. About the time he hits the floor and runs past me I turn to find Mom standing there.

"So the surface people need our help?" I put my hands back on my hips to let her know I disapprove. She sighs.

"Sam, It sounds like they are pretty bitter over everything and I'm not really sure how this is going to go but when Matthew asked I had to come up with some age appropriate way of explaining things okay?" She shrugs as if it's no big deal.

"How did you know they were sending Kate before I did?"

"Honey... look they decided that the minute you two came back and debriefed them. They just didn't want a fight with you so they waited until they were ready for her to leave to tell you." Mom glances over my shoulder at the door, as if scared someone would overhear her explaining it to me.

"Maybe I would be less confrontational if people would start letting me in on things and stop treating me like a child!" My feet swish against the concrete floor as I turn and stomp my way back out.

"Where are you going?" Mom calls after me, clearly concerned I'll run off again or something. Still doesn't trust me... Apparently trust is something everyone is short on these days...

"To find something to eat... and a place to be alone." I growl.

'I just hope Kate gets back quick...' I think to myself as I shove the double doors open again and make my exit.

Chapter Seventeen

It's been three days. Kate is still gone and everyone is getting nervous. I had tried talking to dad and offering to lead a team to go after her but of course he said it was too dangerous. He isn't going to risk mine or anyone else's safety at this point. We don't know if something happened to Kate or if negotiations are just lasting a while or what...

Suddenly someone comes pounding down the stairs, "Doctor Overton! Doctor Overton!" A face appears from the corridor, breathing heavily. It's Megan. I smirk as she stops to catch her breath, hands on her knees.

"What is it Megan? See a scary monster?" I giggle and she rolls her eyes.

"I need your dad. Not you. Last time I checked you weren't a doctor, just a freak." She shoves past me and bangs on the lab door impatiently.

It opens just enough for a gray haired man to poke his head through. He scans Megan up and down.

"What's the matter, Miss?" His eyes glance back in my direction briefly before resettling on Megan.

"A bird showed up carrying a message! It's outside. We haven't read it yet though. I rushed down to tell Doctor Overton." She smiles proudly as if she just saved the day.

I gasp and turn to head outside. My dad's voice wavers over my shoulder, "Sam! Wait. Let us check this out first." I cringe but stop, allowing him to walk by me before following close behind. A few other members of NASA and some regular people follow curiously.

On the surface Megan quickly points in the direction of the large rock I had sat on about a week ago. On top of the boulder rests a large bird. It looks like what I remember a hawk looks like, only... different. Its feathers seem to shimmer as if reflective. The bird lets out a long squawk that sounds like nothing I've ever heard before. Tied to the bird's foot with a thin green vine appears to be a rolled up piece of paper.

My dad approaches the bird cautiously, the hawk, if that is what it is, appears uninterested. Dad slowly reaches for the bird, and once sure it means him no harm, he tugs the vine loose and grabs the message. The bird instantly flys off.

I watch dad's face as he reads the words on the paper. His face goes pale and the note slips from his hands and hits the ground. He trudges past me in a daze, reminding me of something from an old zombie movie. Everyone watches him with big eyes, scared to speak or even move.

I break the stillness by diving for the message. Dad doesn't try to stop me. He just marches down the stairs and out of sight. With the message in my hand I read the words out loud.

"Underworlders, we have your messenger. Please understand that due to previous events, namely what occurred before the asteroid strike, our council has voted not to trust your kind. We have an obligation to our people here on the surface. We will protect our own, particularly from the likes of you. You will stay away from our city and our people. To show you that we are serious we have taken your messenger captive. She will remain with us and serve us here. She will be treated humanely so long as our request is met. There will be no peace negotiations. We consider your people terrorists. Stay on your side of the woods or you will be sorry. We will not hesitate to defend our land and people." ~ The Overworlders.

My stomach hurts and I think I might throw up. I look around and realize everyone has the same fear in their eyes. There's a pause as it all sets in before everyone turns and heads back inside, without a word.

After a moment I follow them, tucking the note into my pocket. When I enter the bedroom area it's a buzz with whispers. As I approach our bunks I notice Sara cradling Matthew. It's too quiet to hear but from the way his back is moving I can tell he's sobbing. His mom looks up at me, her eyes pleading for me to give her some kind of hope.

I have nothing.

Kate's been taken captive. The overworlders see us as a threat and won't negotiate peace. I may never see Shane again...

I crawl onto my bed, roll over away from Sara and Matty, and cry.

'This can't be happening...'

Chapter Eighteen

"Sammy?"

I'm tiptoeing towards the door when a soft whisper causes me to stop in my tracks.

"Shoot..." I mutter under my breath and slowly turn around. Matthew is standing there rubbing his eyes sleepily.

"It's okay Matty. Go back to bed." I try to usher him back but he just tilts his head in confusion.

"Where are you going?" He glances at the flashlight in my hand and then back up at my face.

I sigh. There's no way he's just going to drop it... maybe I can at least convince him not to tell anyone until morning... by then I should be back anyway.

"I'm going to go find my friend and ask him to help Kate."

Matthew's eyes get big, "Can he bring her home?"

"I don't know. Maybe... Don't you think we owe it to Kate to at least try everything we can?" He nods.

"Okay..." I glance back over his shoulder and nod towards the door to the sleeping area, "So go back to bed alright? I should be back in a few hours."

"Okay Sammy..." he yawns and turns to head back to bed.

"And Matty..." he twists his head back to look at me as I finish,

"this is just between us okay?"

He nods and disappears behind the double doors, letting it swing softly shut behind him. I turn and climb the stairs up and out of the bunker. It's dark out and a low fog hangs in the air, making it difficult to see more than a few feet in front of me. Maybe this isn't the best idea... but I don't have any others.

It's funny how the stars seem to be the only things that haven't really changed. As I head towards the woods I can't help but search the sky above for the constellations. They are all right where I remember them. But they soon disappear as I slip under the canopy of trees.

The forest at night is a noisy place, only adding to its eeriness. The hoots of owls and the cries of coyotes ring out, most likely all genetically mutated like the squirrel and hawk... I can only imagine how much more dangerous some of them must be now considering how dangerous they were before...

It's cold out tonight. A breeze keeps drifting through the woods around me, rustling leaves and giving my arms goosebumps. I finally make it to the other side, bursting out of the tree line in relief. My heart is beating out of my chest. I double over wheezing for a moment, realizing that for the last little bit I must have been holding my breath in fear.

I make my way through the city, careful to stay in the shadows, despite the fact that I know everyone is probably asleep this time of night. Can't be too careful. If I'm caught, who knows what that'll mean for Kate... The storm cellar doors are just ahead and I pray he's here. I'm not sure if this is just a meeting place or where he stays.

Crouched down beside the doors I glance around to make sure no one is nearby. Should I knock? Just yank it open? What even is the protocol for a hole in the ground?

I decide to knock. My hand curls into a fist and I bring it down hard on the door a few times. It suddenly bursts open knocking me backwards. Someone grabs me by my foot and jerks me down. My butt bounces down a few stairs as the doors slam shut overhead. It's too dark to see, even with our enhanced night vision, and I think my flashlight got left outside.

"Are you crazy?" The voice hisses at me in a whisper. A hand grabs mine and pulls me to my feet, leading me down the stairs.

When we round the corner at the bottom there's light again. And I can clearly see Shane, his hand still in mine. I start to blush at the thought of holding his hand but then I see his face. He does not look happy...

"I... uh..." He releases my hand and I use it to rub my other arm nervously, "Your people took Kate..."

"I'm aware. And I'm also aware that you were warned that if any of you come here she'd be in big trouble. Are you trying to get your friend killed?"

My mouth drops open slightly at that word.

"Killed?! What the heck is wrong with you people?" I stare at him, shocked, as he shakes his head.

"We people? Look I don't get a say in things around here but are your people any better after what they did to us?"

I get quiet. He has a point.

Shane sighs. "Up here we take care of our own. It's... the motto of our people. The council will do whatever they feel will protect all of us from any threat. And they see you and your people as the threat. You won't be able to negotiate with them. Cassie and I can try to voice our opinion and vouch for you... But like I said we don't really have much of a say."

"They kidnapped Kate and they are apparently willing to kill her... And they see us as the bad guys?"

He shrugs and hangs his head. Suddenly the doors burst open again and we both jerk our heads around. I gasp and run behind Shane, who holds his arm out as if telling me to stay there. From around the corner emerges a group of about five bodies.

"Da...dad?" I step out from behind Shane, confusion settling in.

My father steps forward and I glance behind him to see a lime green body being held by Megan.

"What are you..." I start but Shane interrupts.

"Cassie?" His voice rises and he starts to dive at my dad, who shoves him back pretty effortlessly. Sure enough, it's Cassie. Her arms are tied behind her and she has a gag in her mouth. She doesn't look like she's been hurt but she doesn't look happy.

I help Shane to his feet but he pushes me off, as if he believes I had something to do with it.

"Dad, what are you doing? Let her go!" I yell at him in a rage. He shakes his head somberly.

"No, I'm sorry Samantha but this is the only way."

"You followed me? How did you even know I was going? Did Matthew tell you?"

He shakes his head, "No, I figured you'd try something like this. I know you. We found this one following you through the woods." He glances over at Shane this time and continues, "Shane, good to see you survived. I'm genuinely glad for that. Now I'm going to need you to do me a favor. I'd like you to please inform whoever it is that's in charge here that we have one of you and we want to do a prisoner exchange. Tomorrow. High noon. How about in the place you and Samantha were first reunited?"

Shane looks at me and studies my eyes. He seems to sense I truly had no part in it and reaches over to squeeze my hand before nodding at my father.

"Good. Samantha, let's go. Shane, we will see you tomorrow. This doesn't have to be a war, you know?" My dad and his crew turn to leave and I slowly file in behind them.

"Let's hope not..." Shane mutters. My dad glances over his shoulder at him one last time, a look of concern flickers across his face only briefly, but I saw it. And I know he's afraid. He's afraid he may have started just that.

Chapter Nineteen

I'm dragging my feet behind my father as we head towards the meeting place. Tensions were high all night as everyone worried about how today would go. They had given Cassie a bunk to sleep on but they had round the clock watch on her all night. Not that she was going to try to run. I watch her moving with her head held high ahead of my dad, her hands still bound. She isn't scared at all. It honestly amazes me the amount of composure she can have in a situation like this...

Walking through the woods with our group I notice the handle of a gun sticking out of my dad's back pocket. I narrow my eyes in disapproval but it doesn't really surprise me. He's prepared for the worst. I glance around at Megan and Andy and the others. It's almost always the same team. The only ones willing to volunteer I suppose.

We're coming up on the meeting place and it seems the overworlders have beat us here. A mass of iridescent green stands out amongst the darkened wood of the trees. All except for one body... a softer yellow...

Kate.

I noticed that the area around her right eye is a brown color. She has a black eye... I glance up at my dad and I can tell by the look on his face he's noticed it as well. We come to a stop about 20 paces away from them and he decides to address this observation.

"So do your people consider giving someone a black eye humane?"

I stand up on my tippy toes, trying to get a better look at the crowd of overworlders. Shane doesn't appear to be with them... He must have just told them how to get here. Why wouldn't he come? The woman standing at the front of their group, the one holding Kate's restraints, responds.

"I believe our message stated that so long as none of you crossed onto our side of the forest that she would be treated humanely. And after last night's stunt, you're lucky it's nothing more than a black eye." The woman rolls her eyes as if the whole conversation is beneath her.

"All we wanted was peace. You drove us to this by kidnapping Kate. All we want is to get her back. And we didn't harm Cassie. Did we Cassie?" Dad nudges her on the arm slightly and she shakes her head.

The woman holding Kate huffs, frustrated. "Let's just get on with things. We release them both on the count of three."

"And then we return to our sides of the forest? No more kidnapping or conflict?" There's suspicion in my father's voice. And judging by the hesitation from the other side, he's right to be suspicious.

Shane had told me about how their leader was a woman named Carter who used to be the chemistry professor. This woman must be her. She nods in response to my father's question but it's a slow nod, as if she's not sure of it. I don't like the way it looks and I can tell my dad doesn't either. But comfortable with it or not we have no choice but to trust it if we want to get Kate back.

"Alright then... You start the count." My dad glances at me nervously and his eyes dart back behind him, as if insisting I get back. He's expecting trouble. And he's probably right. So I do as he suggested and I step behind him.

"One." A shout rings out from the overworlders.

"Two." My father shouts.

"Three."

I can't tell who said the last number. As soon as it rang out Kate and Cassie both took off running. After that everything seemed to happen so fast. The overworlders suddenly had blow darts to their mouths, aimed at us. My dad's gun was up and facing Dr. Carter. The woods suddenly became extremely quiet as everybody stood there just staring at each other... waiting for someone to make the first move.

"You are outnumbered." Her voice rings out, breaking the silence.

"Bullets travel faster than darts." My dad mutters. His free hand reaches back to make sure I'm safely behind him.

Carter opens her mouth to speak again but suddenly there's a loud crack of what sounds like thunder in the distance behind us. All of the overworlders' heads jerk to the sky, eyes wide in what appears to be terror.

Dr. Carter gasps and turns to her people, "RUN!"

And just like that there's a streak of green disappearing into the woods.

"What the?" Andy mutters, confused, next to me.

My dad turns around, his face pale from the intensity of the situation, and says, "I don't know... but if they are running... Maybe we should be too."

And with that we all take off towards the bunker in a panic.

As we reach the edge of the woods and break out into the clearing on the open street I look out into the distance. There appears to be a wall of rust colored rain getting closer and closer. The bunker is ahead about midway between us and the rain.

"What the heck is that?!" I scream towards my dad as we run.

He shakes his head. "Get inside! Everyone hurry!"

We all slide into the bunker just as the rain is almost upon us. My dad's the last one in and he tries to pull the door shut but slips and tumbles down the stairs. I rush over to him to make sure he's okay but he's already getting up. Andy yells out about the door being open. Suddenly there's a scream behind me and I jerk my head around. Andy is at the top of the stairs yanking the door shut and screaming in pain. The door closes and he stumbles down the stairs still screaming, holding his arm. Suddenly he passes out and smacks to the floor with a sickening thunk.

Everyone rushes over and I push my way through, falling to my knees next to him. My dad and Kate elbow their way in as well, insisting that I get back. Dad rolls him over and everyone leans in to look at his arm. There's a collective gasp around the room.

His arm is covered in blotches... but the skin around the blotches has turned from yellow back to tan. It's like the rain washed away his new skin tone and reverted his arm back to its original color. "Is that... is that even possible?" I glare at my father, demanding an answer. Suddenly all eyes are on him, waiting to see just what he'll say.

He looks completely lost as he continues to stare at the unconscious Andy. "It shouldn't be. And if I know anything for sure... It's that this is not a good thing..."

He looks around and gestures for the nurse. My dad and a few other men help carry Andy's body to the infirmary room. I follow them.

"I want to know everything. He needs to be under observation at all times. If the rain did somehow... I don't know... Burn the radiation out of his arm... His body won't be able to handle it properly. The vaccine rewrote our DNA so that our bodies would absorb the radiation and adapt to it. We need the radiation that's in us now for our body to function properly. I have the feeling that unless this is only temporary... It's going to make him very very sick..."

"That's why they ran. They've seen this before..." I mutter and my dad turns to me, a look of agreement in his eyes.

"That's what I'm afraid of... They knew to be scared. So what exactly is this?" It was a rhetorical question so I don't bother answering, not that I would have any idea how to answer that anyway. My dad and I stand there, silently staring at our unconscious friend. After a moment my father pats me on the shoulder, no doubt in an attempt to console me, and then leaves without another word.

Chapter Twenty

When the doors to the living quarters open and Dad walks through he's instantly mobbed by curious residents. He doesn't seem to mind though, it's clear he's there to make an announcement anyway. After a good crowd has formed dad starts in.

"Okay everyone, I know we're all concerned about the reaction Andrew... Andy... had to the rain. It's clear that we will need to avoid going out during any rainstorms. It appears the acid in the rain can literally burn the radiation from our skin. Being that we need the radiation to survive now this is a problem." A rumble of whispers breaks out but dad holds up his hand to calm it down. The people hush again and dad goes on. "We at NASA have been working tirelessly through the night and we have created an antidote."

Cheers erupt and dad lets them quiet down on their own before continuing this time.

"Thank you. But it is experimental obviously. We are going to be administering an injection of it to Andy momentarily. If his body reacts positively we expect him to wake up within the hour and hopefully recover in a day or two. But we can't make any promises at the moment... So, if you are a praying person, I'm sure Andrew would appreciate it. Thanks." Dad turns around and pushes his way back through the group towards the doors again.

Suddenly a voice close behind me makes me jump slightly.

"Shouldn't YOU be in there when he wakes?"

I turn to find Megan, hands on hips, behind me: an accusing look on her face.

"You can't seriously be blaming me for acid rain..." My eyes widen at the suggestion.

"No. But you have to admit... There's a reason we were all out there. But regardless of who's fault it may or may not be... Don't you know Andy likes you?" Her eyebrow raises as if she really can't believe I was unaware.

I was unaware...

"What?" My face goes warm again. I'm getting used to that feeling at this point. Megan grins, amused at my embarrassment, or at the fact that she knew something before I did... Probably both honestly.

"Why do you think he's been volunteering for everything involving you?" She glances at her nails and then raises them to her mouth to cover a yawn.

"Well, if that was an indicator of a crush then I'd have some questions for you too Megan." I give her a teasing look of concern. She is mid yawn when I say it and she actually begins to cough and sputter with surprise. Now her face is going orange like mine. I snicker a bit but try to hide it.

"Hilarious." She grumbles, after clearing her throat. "But whatever. Believe me or don't." She pushes past me with a huff and out the door.

Whether she was just trying to get in my head or not... I guess I do owe it to Andy in some way to be there. I don't know... So I make my way to the infirmary. As I push through the heavy door a couple nurses hop out of the way. They give me a small look of

annoyance but don't question my presence. There are only about six hospital type beds in the room each with a gray curtain for privacy. Most of the curtains are open and the beds empty. Only two curtains are closed. I notice dad is already here again as well. Back in the far corner of the room, next to one of the curtains, his back is to me as he whispers to the doctor.

I assume the curtain by them must be Andy's and I start moving towards it. The doctor makes eye contact with me from behind my dad and nods at me. This causes dad to turn around and scan the room, noticing me. His eyes narrow but he gives me a slow nod of approval and tilts his head towards the curtain, as if giving me permission to go inside. I do.

I pull the fabric back, the sound of metal scraping metal above my head makes me cringe, although I'm not sure why. It's not like he's taking a nap and I might wake him. I'm sure everyone would be relieved if noisy curtain hooks were enough to wake him. As I turn towards his bed I can't help but look at his arm first. Blotches of tan skin cover his arm, bigger than before now. I'm fascinated by them. It's been years since anyone had seen that color skin before... Suddenly the curtain on the other side jerks open and I about jump out of my own skin. Dad marches over with the doctor in step right behind him. They ignore me.

"Ready?" My father looks at the doctor who I now see is holding a small needle with a brownish liquid inside. He nods in response but says nothing.

I stare silently as the doctor uses an alcohol wipe to sterilize Andy's upper arm before administering the shot. I watch as the plunger slowly depresses and the liquid drains from the vial into Andy's arm. I don't know what I expected to happen exactly. Would Andy bolt upright awake? Would he start shaking and convulsing? Would he gasp or his eyes flutter open gently?

But none of those things happened. The beeping from his monitor didn't change. His body remained motionless and there wasn't a hint of movement to his eyes. His breath remained slow and steady and really, nothing changed at all. The doctor placed a Band-Aid on Andy's arm and exited the small curtain walled room. I looked to dad for reassurance. He met my eyes and seemed to notice my concern.

"It's not going to happen immediately, Sam. Give it some time. I have to go..."

The look on his face was angry and fearful. Which can't mean anything good. But investigating his intentions will have to wait. My friend needs me here. I drag a small metal folding chair over closer and plop down into it. Dad had told the assembly that he hoped it wouldn't take more than an hour. I can wait that long. What could happen in an hour?

.....

It's been 75 minutes according to the small round analog clock on the back wall. My foot is tapping uncontrollably. It's been too long. I stand up and pull back the curtain, looking around for anyone. A nurse walks out of the other curtained room nearby. I still don't know who is in that one or for what reason but at the moment I don't really care.

"Hey, nurse?" I call her and she glances back at me, annoyed.

"What is it?" She sighs.

"Um, I was just... I mean, it's been over an hour and my dad thought..." before I can finish, a noise behind me catches my attention.

"Sa..."

I whip around and see Andy's eyes opening slightly. "Nurse! He's waking up!" I shout and footsteps come racing. She's likely going to find the doctor or my dad. I rush to Andy's side as he groans and begins to move.

"Sam?" He questions.

"Yeah, it's me. You're okay..."

"My arm hurts." His voice is soft and raspy.

"Yeah... I uh, I can get the doctor..." I start to turn away but he reaches out with his good arm and grabs my hand. "No, wait, stay. Please?" He lets go of my hand and looks embarrassed. I nod slowly and turn back to him but now I'm a little uncomfortable. What Megan had told me replays in my head and I glance behind me at the curtain nervously.

Andy notices.

"I'm sorry... if I freaked you out... I just don't want to be alone. You know?"

I nod. "I get it..."

"So, um, what happened anyway?" He asks, trying to push himself up into a more upright position. His eyes land on his arm and go wide. "What's wrong with my arm?"

"You uh, the acid rain, like, sucked the radiation out of your arm or something like that. They gave you a shot and..." the sound of the curtain being pulled back shuts me up.

My dad, the nurse, the doctor, and a couple others from NASA burst in. Dad gives me the "go away" look and I oblige, slipping out without another word. At least I know he's okay. Now I have to figure out what to do about this war that's coming...

Chapter Twenty One

"Where the heck do you think you're going?"

I stop in my tracks just a few feet from the double doors and cringe. Slowly turning on my heels I face her. Why does she always show up at the worst times?

"Shh..." I hiss. "You're going to wake someone." I glance around the room at all the bunks nearby. Nobody stirs.

Megan glares at me, hands on her hips, grumpy as usual.

"Well?" She demands an answer.

"You know good and well where I'm going."

"You're an idiot."

I sigh, "Did you stop me just to tell me that or are you planning on tattling on me?"

She makes a face as if to say 'Tattling? Really? What are we five?'. But then she seems to mull it over a moment. "What I'm going to do is go back to bed. You aren't worth the lack of sleep." She turns around and starts to march back to her bunk.

"Hey Megan..." she pauses but doesn't look back, "Thanks." Still facing away from me she huffs, "I'm not doing it for you. If you aren't back by breakfast I'm spilling my guts to Kate first thing." Then she slinks off into the shadows.

I shake my head and gently push open one of the doors just enough to slip through. When I climb the stairs to the main exit I only open a tiny crack at first and peer out. The last thing I wanna do is fling it open wide to find it raining again. But thankfully the sky appears clear. The moon a crescent shape tonight gives off an unnatural hue... sort of a pale teal or seafoam essence. As I climb out of the hatch and very carefully close it back behind me without letting it make more than a soft click, I can't help but take a moment to marvel at the moon above.

But after a moment I remember my mission and snap out of it.

I've got to find Shane and Cassie and figure out what we can do to fix this feud. It's not good for either side. I head off towards the woods, moving somewhat slowly so that my feet won't make noise pounding against the ground below. I can't alert anyone from either side that I'm out, especially that I'm heading for overworlder territory.

There's a howl in the distance and freeze. A wolf? A coyote? A dog? Something besides squirrels and bugs actually survived out here? Remembering how big that squirrel Shane shot was brings an uneasiness into my stomach as I walk. If a squirrel had grown that much... imagine what a wolf might look like now... I pick up the pace. A sound behind me makes me gasp and I glance back over my shoulder.

Nothing there. Nothing I can see anyway.

Cringing, I put my feet into overdrive. At least if an overworlder finds me I'd have a better chance at gaining some mercy. No animal is going to hesitate. Of course, at this point I'm not so sure a human would for long either. I make it to the city's edge and stop behind the nearest tree to look out. There are a couple people walking around. They definitely appear to have been placed here as lookouts. Obviously the president lady didn't want to risk us sneaking back in like I'm trying to do. But with only two, as far as I can see, she must not have thought a threat was imminent tonight. Not that I'm a threat to them anyway. Although she probably wouldn't agree.

I wait for a while. Looking for the perfect opening. One of the guards heads around a building corner on the far side. The other turns around to watch as his partner disappears. I take the chance while I have it and bolt for the nearest building. There's a fire escape ladder on the side and I leap for it. The ladder shakes a little and I wince at the small sound it makes. But I don't risk waiting to find out if it was heard. I swiftly climb to the roof and roll onto it. From here I can see the roof of Shane's place not that far away. All I have to do now is get to it without being seen. I sigh and slowly move over to the edge nearest that direction.

I glance down and around. There's another building close enough and it doesn't look like any guards in sight of the alley between. So I jump. I hit the other roof hard and hold my breath, laying flat for a moment to listen for voices. Nothing. I army crawl to the next edge just to be safe and peek over. There's someone below. I pull my head back and lay face down again. I'm nervous to pull my head back up, because I don't want to risk being spotted, but I know there's no other way. I can't just stay on this roof forever. So I peer over again. Gone.

But maybe not far... I sit there a moment, staring at the next roof. What if I hit hard again and that person is still close by? What if they hear me? Maybe I should just go bolting across them and hope for the best. If I make it to Shane's, even if I'm spotted, maybe he can vouch for me... Of course, he wasn't at the exchange... What if he's not even here? Or what if he's sick or something and can't help me? Or what he's mad about Cassie and blames me and decides to just not?

My breath is getting fast and my chest tightens. I'm giving myself a panic attack. Great. I can't do this right now. I've gotta just make a decision and go with it. I stand up, bounce in place a few times to work up the nerve, and then soar. One roof, two roofs, three roofs, Shane's. I hit the pavement and glance around only briefly.

Nobody is close by. No yelling and no footsteps. I made it. It's fine.

This is fine.

I don't even bother knocking on Shane's door because I'm in such a tizzy. I just grab the knob and twist it right open. Rushing inside I turn back, I'm surprised it wasn't locked but I'm not making that same mistake. I pull it shut quickly and twist the little lock latch, testing the knob once more to be sure it locked properly.

"Sam? What the heck?!" Spinning on my heels I face a very sleepy, and not fully clothed, Shane. He has on some linen knee length boxers with what appears to be shamrocks on them and a white cotton tank top. His hair is sticking up on the right side and he's rubbing his face as if trying to wake himself up. Meanwhile, I'm blushing again. I glance down and then around, trying to avert my eyes because seeing him in his underwear makes me incredibly uncomfortable. He doesn't seem to notice though as he flips on a lamp and stretches with a yawn.

"You're crazy." He mutters as he walks behind me towards the door. "Did anyone see you?"

"No, I mean... I don't..." before I can finish the door flings open and a figure slips in. Shane jumps a little and holds his hand out behind him, very protective like. It would make me smile if I weren't currently concerned with who might be barging in this late. Maybe someone had seen me... But no, it's only Cassie. She glances at Shane and seems completely unbothered by the fact that he's in his underwear. A fact that makes my chest tighten a little in what I assume is jealousy. Is this a regular thing for them? Why wouldn't it bother her and why is she here so late and does she have a key and... Her eyes make contact with mine and narrow.

"Well, that explains it." A soft sigh escapes her lips and she shakes her head.

"Explains what?!" It comes out a little defensive because I'm not sure what she's thinking. I can see how my being in Shane's house in the middle of the night with him in his underwear could probably look bad... but...

"This." She steps out of the shadows and motions behind her. Soft thuds follow and a small silhouette appears.

"Crap." Shane mutters quietly and looks back at me, his eyes full of questions and maybe an accusation or two as well.

I'm actually pretty speechless for a moment but finally regain my composure and gasp, eyes wide.

"Matty?"

"Hey Sammy..." he looks down at the floor and shuffles his feet nervously.

"What are you doing here? How did you even find this place? This is so dangerous!"

"I... I followed you... I just wanted to help you." He looks up and I can already see tears trailing slowly down his cheeks. "Are you mad at me?"

I rush over to him and kneel down, wrapping my arms around him in a hug. "No. Not mad. But it's not safe out here and I don't know what I'd do if you got hurt." His little hands squeeze me as tightly as he can.

At this point Cassie speaks up again, "Yeah. Better be glad I found him before a guard did."

I glance over at her again. She's trying to look bored but I can tell by her shoulders she's stressed. "Thanks Cassie. I know... I know it probably wasn't easy for you to help him after..."

"I don't want to talk about it." She snaps, interrupting me. I nod. "Okay."

"I'm not a savage. He's a child. What was I supposed to do?" She stomps past me and heads for Shane's fridge.

This reminds me that Shane is still in the room somewhere. I glance around to look for him. When my gaze finds him I'm a little surprised to see he's now dressed, sitting on the couch. He's pulled on a pair of blue jeans that must have been lying on the floor nearby somewhere. He still has the white tank top on but now he has a black leather jacket, unzipped, over it. He's watching me silently, his hair still sticking up a little on that one side. I wait for him to say something or lecture me about Matthew but he doesn't. He slips on his tennis shoes lying on the floor in front of him and bounces up off the couch, patting his thighs as if to say 'alright then, let's get going'.

"I wanted to talk about yesterday..." I say.

He shakes his head. "We need to get y'all out of here."

"But we have to find a way to make peace between our people or things could get out of hand..."

"They already are Sam." He moans and rubs the back of his head.

"What do you mean?" I'm confused and I'm sure that it shows on my face.

"Look, I don't know who started it yesterday... but after everybody ended up pulling weapons on each other..." he glances over at Cassie as if double checking his words with her. She nods and he continues, "President Smith ordered those guards to shoot on sight."

I'm absolutely appalled but manage to stammer out, "Wait... wha... what?" Shaking slightly, Matthew grabs my leg. Scared. I don't blame him. "How can she do that? What kind of people are these people?!" Anger rises up in me and it's reflected in the pitch of my voice.

"Shhh..." Shane looks uncomfortable. "My people Sam. Listen, I get it. I agree with you. They're overreacting..."

"Overreacting? This goes beyond overreacting. This is insane! It's... it's barbaric." I grind my teeth, trying to calm myself down, if only for Matty's sake. I drop an arm to rub his back, reassuring him. The shaking stops but his head is still buried in my leg.

"You're not wrong." Shane is quiet for a moment as if thinking it over. Cassie stares at us from the kitchen bar stool she has climbed up on, a half eaten sandwich of some kind in her hand. She doesn't offer an opinion, only listens. Shane continues, "and that's exactly why we need to get you both back home... now."

He grabs my hand and practically drags me to the door. The second my body starts moving I wrap my other hand around Matty's, pulling him alongside. There's a thump behind us and then footsteps, Cassie following us apparently. Outside we slip between buildings and behind dumpsters and other random objects trying to avoid being seen. Shane still has hold of my hand as we go.

Occasionally, I think I feel him brushing his thumb across it tenderly but it's so quick that I wonder if I'm simply imagining it.

This is no time for daydreaming' I think to myself, trying to snap out of it.

"Okay" Shane's voice makes me jump slightly as it cuts through the silence. He points at the tree line up ahead. "We're going to have to make a run for it." Letting go of my hand he holds his out in kind of a 'wait for it' gesture. He watches a guard a ways down and the moment the man disappears around a building's edge he throws his hand forward and whispers "run!"

We make a mad dash for the tree line. But Matty can't keep up with us. I have his hand but I'm practically dragging him so I stop to scoop him up into my arms.

"Hey!" Voices behind us screech out and our legs kick it into over-drive. But it's not enough. A streaking pain hit my left shoulder blade and I scream, losing my balance and tumbling to the dirt. Matty is thrown from my arms and he begins to cry. "Mat..." I try to reach out for him but there looks to be two of him and I'm not sure which to reach for. Shane and Cassie, or well... a couple of each of them, race back towards us and Shane's strong arms lift me into the air. After that I slip in and out of consciousness.

Shane carries me while Cassie carries Matty. Shane and I are ahead. When we reach the edge on our people's side Cassie calls out. When Shane turns around he sees Matthew running up and past him towards the bunker door. Cassie is still back at the tree line, shaking her head.

"I'm not going back in there Shane."

"I understand." His chest vibrates a little when he says it.

"You really shouldn't either." Her voice shakes some when she says it.

"Be safe Cassie. They might have identified us... Smith won't be happy we helped them."

She sighs. "I'll be fine. You're the one I'm worried about." She turns to leave and Shane watches her go for a moment. Suddenly there's a loud clang and voices behind him and he spins on his heel.

My dad and a few others explode out of the bunker entrance. Dad yanks me from Shane's arms. He's yelling but I can't understand any of it really. Finally he nods his head, a look of concern on his face, and Shane is allowed to walk in with us.

Chapter Twenty Two

Dr. Overton rushed inside with his daughter nestled tightly in his strong arms. People began to fall in behind him, pushing one another to see what was going on. Nearby Matthew cries in his mother's arms as he rambles on about what had happened, obviously blaming himself. But it's not his fault. Someone should tell him that... it's not his fault, it's theirs. The overworlders. They did this.

The thought reminds him of the fact that one is now in their midst. He glances sideways at Shane, eyes narrowed, but says nothing. He pushes through the double doors to the infirmary and rushes to the nearest bed, quickly placing Samantha down on it. She's completely unconscious at this point.

"Tell me what I need to know!" He growls at Shane as he grabs a couple latex gloves from the box nearby and pulls them on.

Rolling Sam over gently he examines the wound. The actual puncture itself isn't very large, only about a centimeter in diameter, but that's not really his main concern. The area around the opening in her skin has turned dark purple, thick black lines trace off in multiple directions and seem to be slowly growing.

"Henbane and..."

"Henbane wouldn't cause this skin discoloration!"

"I wasn't finished... It's a mix of henbane and snake venom." Shane lowers his head as if in submission when Dr. Overton turns to him bewildered.

"What snake?"

"Diamondback rattler."

"Eastern or Western?"

"Um, whichever one lives around here? I don't know..." Shane moves back an inch, nervous around Sam's father.

"Western." James rushes to a cabinet nearby and riffles through bottles. Finally he pulls out a vial labeled 'anti-venom' and reaches for a syringe.

"Uh, the thing is sir... all of the animals had to mutate in order to survive and I'm just not sure if the same anti-venom is going to..." but Dr. Overton was already stabbing the needle in before he could finish. "Well I guess we better hope it does..." Shane mutters, frustrated.

"I can monitor and adjust as needed but it's a start. I also need to get her some physostigmine for the henbane. Why don't you just go sit somewhere back there unless I need you?" He huffs at the young man next to him and points towards a chair near the back wall of the infirmary. Then he watches as his daughter's friend moves back that way, following his directions.

Shane spins the chair around and plants himself in it.

"Psst..."

He lifts his head and glances around curiously.

"Hey, in here." The voice says again.

Shane realizes the sound is coming from behind a nearby curtain and he carefully pulls it back. Andy glances over as the curtain pulls back and lets out a small gasp.

"Um, you must be Sam's friend Shane..."

Shane nods. He'd respond verbally but he's a little in shock staring at Andy's arm. Those blotches... he recognizes that reaction.

"Did you...?" He starts to ask. Seeing the direction of his gaze Andy nods.

"Yeah. Got hit by that rain. Rough stuff."

"To say the least." Shane circles the bed to get a closer look. "How did you survive it?"

Andy's eyebrow raises and Shane adds, "I mean... I've just never seen anyone come through it above. It's just... we don't have a way to treat it I guess."

"Oh..." Andy gets quiet before suddenly changing the subject. "So what's going on out there? Why are you here? No offense..."

Shane shifts his feet, uncomfortable. "Sam, um..."

"Sam?! What happened to Sam?!" Andy tries to sit up and winces before falling back down and angrily clenching his fists. Shane takes a step back and observes. But it doesn't appear Andy is angry with him. It would seem he's angry that he can't get up.

"Do you need some help?" Shane offers.

"No. Thanks. Is Sam okay?" The concern on his face is evident and tells Shane there's something there. Seeing that look in Andy over Sam has some weird feelings stirring up in him now too. Jealousy?

"She got hit with one of our darts..."
"You shot her?!" Andy freaks out.

"No, I didn't shoot her! I saved her!" His face burns and he takes a deep breath, trying to calm himself down. There's no doubt Sam's dad is hearing most of this. It's a wonder he hasn't yelled at them to shut it yet. Andy relaxed a little again.

"So, she'll be okay then?"

Shane glances back around the curtains edge towards Dr. Overton and his daughters still unconscious body. "I hope."

This was not the response Andy was hoping for and Shane clears his throat, "I mean, I'm sure she will. Y'all obviously have a lot of resources here that we don't. I'm sure her dad will have her better in no time..." At this point Shane nods goodbye and closes the curtain, moving back to his chair. He sits and places his head in his hand and sighs.

Shane turns to walk back to his chair, just relieved to see she's awake and okay.

"Shay..." it was muffled and broken but he knew it was meant to be a call for him. He freezes and slowly turns around. Between James and his wife Shane's eyes lock with Sam's and she mumbles it again. James turns to him and nods as they back up a little.

Shane walks back over, gesturing a small 'thank you' at her parents with his eyes as he slips up beside her and takes her hand in his.

Chapter Twenty Four

When I had woken up there was searing pain, bright lights, weird noises, and things attached to my skin that I couldn't identify. So naturally, I panicked. Then I saw Shane... and I saw the concern in his eyes... At first it made it worse. I thought the concern he had was the same as mine. But hearing his voice I realized that his concern was with my reaction, not my surroundings. He needed me to calm down. I needed to calm down. And I tried. But the pain was still there. When my parents came in I understood where I was and what was happening. A cooling sensation enters my wrist and I glance down to find an IV. Morphine. The pain subsided almost instantly and with it my hysteria as well.

I try to call for Shane but my voice is too weak. Thankfully he hears me anyway and comes back. Warmth radiates off his palm as he grabs my hand gently in his. It feels nice. Under different circumstances I might be blushing but, under the influence of the painkillers, I just grin, giddy over it.

"Samantha," my dad says from somewhere behind me. I hadn't even noticed that he'd moved. I twist my head slightly to look back at him. "I'm going to need to roll you up on your side to check your wound and replace the bandage." "Shane?" I question him.

Dad nods. "Yes, Shane can stay where he is." I turn back to Shane and smile. He gives me an unsure grin back. Then my dad and the nurse are lifting me up. It's uncomfortable but the morphine must really be doing its job because the pain has pretty much disappeared completely.

Shane glances over my shoulder, the curiosity getting the better of him. It's obvious that he instantly regrets it. His face goes pale and he jerks his eyes away. The reaction causes my stomach to flop.

"Is it bad?" I mutter, nauseous.

Shane won't answer nor meet my eyes. Dad isn't so hesitant.

"Well, the fact that you woke up within just a few hours means that the physostigmine is probably doing its job against the henbane." His tone is curious and focused.

"Henbane?" I question.

"Poisonous plant. Many years ago it was used in combination with other plants as a natural anesthesia. But it can be very deadly when not properly adjusted and controlled. During the middle ages it was actually nicknamed the witches herb for that very reason. It was mixed with snake venom in the dart they hit you with."

Shane glances up at my dad but immediately looks away again. This time his face reflected shame instead of disgust. Dad must have given him an accusing look. I squeeze his hand softly and he squeezes back, acknowledging my attempt to comfort him.

"Anyway," my father continues behind me, "the wound itself is superficial. The infection is my main concern. You're going to have some temporary muscle and tissue damage... hmm... I think I'm gonna go ahead and give you another dose of the anti-venom. And..."

His voice trails off, his finger tracing a line a little lower on my back than where the actual wound is.

"What?" I ask.

"Maryann?" He addresses my mom this time. "Do you remember what age she was last time she got a tetanus shot?"

"Oh wow... umm, twelve? That ER visit during youth group?" Her voice doesn't seem confident but dad accepts this answer.

"Okay. So that shouldn't be an issue but I'm going to go ahead and give her a booster just in case. But I don't like this line here."

His finger begins tracing again and I assume he's showing mom and the nurse a "line" of some kind on my back. I know enough to know a red line coming from a wound can indicate blood poisoning. I've had it once before and I have always watched for the line ever since.

"I'm going to start her on Ceftriaxone as well. It's an antibiotic to combat sepsis." He tapes a new pad onto my back before laying me back down. He pats me on the shoulder. "You'll be alright. But you need to rest and stay close to the infirmary for the next three to five days. Minimum."

I don't like it but I nod, "Okay." To be honest, I can barely move my arm on that side, I doubt I'd be much use anywhere else right now anyway. The nurse leaves a moment and returns with two needles. She raises up my bed until I'm in a sitting position and then she sticks my arm, both shots back to back. Stab. Stab. I cringe, not because it hurts so much as the fact that I just hate needles. It's like a mental thing. Especially considering a needle put me in here...

"Well, I have work to do. Samantha?" I turn towards dads voice and he waits until my eyes find him to finish, "Get some rest okay? Try?"

I nod again but say nothing. He leaves and just behind him mom does too. The nurse writes a few things down on a clipboard at the end of my bed and then she's gone as well. It's just Shane and I.

"So..." I start, unsure what I'm even going to say. He reaches up and brushes the hair from the side of my face and tucks it behind my ears. His fingers against the skin of my cheeks send a tingling sensation down my jawline. If I had known what I was going to say I definitely wouldn't now. Instead, I just look at him, curious if the gesture was meant as more than what it was.

When he sees the look I'm giving him he pulls his hand away slowly, awkwardly almost. As if he's not even sure if he meant more by it and he's trying to figure that out so he can explain. But just as he opens his mouth to say something there's a loud crash somewhere behind us. I nearly jump out of the bed and into his arms. I can't turn my body around enough to see what happened without hurting myself so I give Shane a "what the heck was that" look. But he isn't looking at me. His gaze is aimed behind me and his face looks super annoyed.

He nods his head at someone behind me and then addresses me, "I'm gonna, um, go find the restroom or something. I'll be back. Some-one wants to talk to you anyway." His eyes shift up again and then he gets up and pushes through the infirmary doors.

A figure appears beside me on the opposite side Shane had been on.

"Uh, hey Sam. Sorry if I startled you... it's my first time trying to get up and move around since before... you know. Anyway, I'll have to apologize to the nurse for breaking that lamp back there I knocked over... if you get up any don't go back that way barefoot for a bit."

It's Andy. I breathe a sigh of relief seeing him looking almost back to normal. Aside from the occasional tan blotch on his arm. But even those seem to have shrunk since the last time I saw him.

"Andy! I'm glad to see you're doing better." I'm actually surprised he was able to get up at all after what he went through.

"Yeah, thanks. Apparently we both need to be more careful huh?" He gestures at me.

"Something like that." I grin.

"Hey, so I wanted to ask you if maybe you'd..." he's blushing and rubbing the back of his head nervously.

I cringe internally but try not to let him see my dismay. 'Please don't', I think to myself, 'Oh gosh, don't let him ask what I think he's going to ask... I really don't want to hurt him...'

Suddenly one of the infirmary doors flies open, hitting the wall behind it with a loud thwack.

"Matthew Daniel!" Sara scolds him as the little pitter patter of feet rush towards me.

"Sammy!" The bed sinks some from the weight as his tiny body leaps up onto me. I groan slightly from the force of the impact but then I laugh. I notice Andy backing away, heading back towards his own curtained "room".

"Matty! I'm so happy to see you buddy!" He has no idea what good timing he has...

His eyes well up with tears as he leans forward and hugs me tight. I wrap him up in my arms and rub his back gently.

"Whoa, I'm okay. No need for tears..." I whisper in his ear and he pulls back to look at me.

"It's my fault though! I shouldn't have followed you." He sniffles and rubs his nose with his sleeve.

I glance over at Sara who's giving me a disapproving scowl. My heart aches and I shake my head. "No bud. It's not your fault. I shouldn't..." I start to say that I shouldn't have gone but I don't really believe that to be true. So instead I just repeat, "It's not your

fault."

Matthew hugs me even tighter and I have to try with all my might not to wince. I don't want to scare him but his squeezing is pulling on the skin of my back some and making my shoulder hurt again. I pat his back and then carefully lift him off of me.

"Thanks for coming to see me, Matty. I'm so glad you're safe." I glance over his shoulder at the door. Sara starts moving a little closer, probably ready to leave. The door has swung back shut by now and isn't moving anymore. Where did Shane go anyway? Just the bathroom? Did he leave? "Um, y'all didn't notice Shane in the auditorium did you?"

Matthew nods his head. "He's still here."

I nod but before I can say more Sara is tugging on Matthew gently.

"Time to go Matthew Honey. It's going to be lunch before long and you need a bath first." Matthew turns to his mom and sighs but accepts her command. He turns back to me and waves goodbye, I smile and return a wave with my uninjured arm.

I probably need to get a nap... but I also want to know where Shane is. My eyelids start to close involuntarily. I try to force them back open but I just don't have the energy to fight it right now. Maybe just a quick nap before lunch. I'm sure Shane will come back soon. At least if I'm asleep maybe Andy won't attempt to talk with me again. I really am not good with this kind of thing. Shane's the only boy I've ever liked... the only one I ever really had much of a chance to like. I don't even know how to entertain thoughts of liking someone else. But the last thing I want to do is hurt anyone else. I remember people used to call it friend-zoning someone. It was always such a negative thing... but what else are you supposed to do when you like someone as a person or a friend but not more?

I'm too tired for all of this.

So tired.

I lean my bed back again and let my eyes close, this time without trying to fight it. A nap couldn't hurt.

Chapter Twenty Five

When Shane left the infirmary he had no idea where he was going to go. He had told Sam the bathroom but he really didn't need it right now. And there really wasn't anywhere else he could go down in the hold with the underworlders anyway. Not his territory, not his to explore. So he sat down right outside the infirmary doors to wait until Andy had a chance to talk with Sam.

That's another thing... Shane had a good idea what Andy wanted to talk to her about. It's the same thing he had wanted to bring up to her himself. These days he's just not used to any kind of competition. Granted, he's not really used to feeling this way about someone either. The last five years have been more about surviving than thriving and finding love.

Is that what this is?

The concrete wall against his back is cold but it's not comfortable to lean forward so he tries to ignore it. A few people walk through the room and most give him uncomfortable glances as they do. It's obvious they are trying hard not to stare. Shane sighs. Maybe he should just go home...

He pushes against the wall and shimmies back up into a standing position. The window on the infirmary door has a small diamond shaped glass and he peers through it, trying not to let his head be in sight in case Andy looks over. Sam is smiling at Andy but her body language looks tense. Andy rubs the back of his head and Shane can see the orange in his face from all the way outside the door.

A grimace forms on his face as he backs away from the window.

He places both hands behind his head and interlocks his fingers.

He turns and places his forehead against the wall beside the door. Maybe he should just go in there? But no. That would be too obvious. Besides, he's not looking to make any more enemies.

But as if on cue an answer appeared.

"You're Sammy's friend. The one that helped us get back." A small voice bellowed out behind him.

He let his arms fall to his side and turned around. It's the kid that followed Sam.

"Uh, yeah. Glad you're okay." Shane nods. Behind the boy is a woman at least ten years older than Shane. The boy's mom no doubt. She gives him a nervous look. The same look he'd been seeing since he arrived. He didn't blame her.

"I was gonna go see her. Is she awake now?" The boy asks, jumping to try to see through the window pane.

"She is." Shane smiles and then it dawns on him, "Actually, I bet she'd really love to see you. I'm sure she was worried about you. You should head on in."

The boy hops excitedly and flings the door open, hard. Shane glances through the open crack before it shuts behind them just in time to catch a glimpse of a retreating Andy. There's only a hint of guilt in him as he turns back around, a slight grin on his face.

"Shane."

His heart, and body, jumps violently at the sound of his name being called. He suddenly feels like he just got caught committing a crime and his stomach flops. Sam's dad is standing in a doorway nearby studying him.

"Sir? You uh... startled me." He lets his head hang and rubs the back of his neck. Hoping the Dr. didn't actually know what he'd just done. Although, he's not sure it could really be considered wrong per se...

"My apologies. I was going to invite you to join us for lunch in the cafeteria."

"I um... I don't..." He stammers, unsure how to respond.

"I insist. Go get cleaned up and you can join us there in half an hour. I put some clothes on the counter in the locker room in the men's restroom for you. You have my daughter's blood on your shirt. And your hands." Dr. Overton turns and disappears back through the door behind him. His voice had sounded friendly enough but that last bit still rang in his ears.

'You have my daughter's blood on... your hands.'

Shane peers down at his hands. He probably should have washed them a long time ago... before breakfast would have been wise. But he'd had other things on his mind then. Although the words were technically true, as he literally did have some remaining dried blood on his hands, they had still felt menacing despite the hospitable tone.

Nonetheless, he proceeds towards the men's restroom to get cleaned up and join Sam's family for lunch, hoping that's all it would be.

~~~~~

Dr. Overton waited just inside the cafeteria doors, watching for their guest to appear. Maryanne, Sara, and Matthew were already sitting at a table nearby with their plates. Eventually the left-hand door cracks a bit and a lime green hand reaches around the edge. Shane quietly pokes through the opening, letting the door swing shut carefully behind him. He looks nervous. Unsurprising.

The boy glances around and instantly ducks his head. Dr. Overton suddenly realizes that the normal cafeteria sounds have ceased. He glasses behind him and instantly understands Shane's reaction. The whole assembly appears to be staring at Shane, their eyes concerned and questioning. James shakes his head in frustration, doesn't anyone know how to behave around here?

"Shane, I'm glad you made it! Thank you for joining us." He welcomes him enthusiastically, hoping his hospitable tone would put his people's minds at ease. The young man may be on overworlder but he's hardly a threat to any of them himself.

Especially not while he's clearly infatuated with Samantha. Besides, he could offer them valuable information if they play their cards right...

The hussle and bussle of eating and conversing returns around them and Shane's shoulders seem to relax a bit. He doesn't say anything in
~~~~~

response to Dr. Overton's welcome but does nod to acknowledge it. Good enough.

James leads Shane to the end of the line and they wait there together. Before reaching the bar and taking a plate he asks his guest,

"You don't have any food allergies do you? If you need an alternative to anything we are serving today we can certainly ma..."

"No. I'm good." Shane interrupts. Then quickly adds, "Um, thanks though."

They each grab a plastic tray and head to the table to join the others. Shane sits down beside Matthew who happily scoots over to make room for him. Sara gives James an uneasy look but he shakes his head slowly, silently asking her not to make a thing of it. She tightens her lips but says nothing, turning her attention back to her half eaten baked potato.

When Dr. Overton turns his attention back to Shane he starts to say something to him but pauses, noticing Shane's head is bowed, his eyes closed, and although he's not making a sound his lips appear to be moving. He watches him curiously. When the boy finishes and looks up at him there's a flush of pink in his cheeks, as if he's been caught doing something strange. And frankly, he's not completely wrong.

"You a religious man?" James questions.

"I am..." Shane hesitates, glancing from face to face. "Are you not?"

Dr. Overton grins, amused. "I am. To a degree."

Matthew then chimes in, "What's relishious?"

"Religious", his mother corrects him and then stares through squinted eyes at Dr. Overton. Warning him to answer her son carefully.

"Oh, yes Matthew... it means to believe in and worship a higher power." James wiggles uncomfortably. Shane notices.

"It means to believe in God." Shane tussles Matthew's hair a little and for the first time since he arrived Sara looks at him a little softer.

"Oh, I believe in God! I talk to Him a lot!" Matthew smiles brightly and then takes a huge bite out of a banana on his plate. "He lubbs ush!"

Sara shakes her head and scolds him. "Matthew. Don't talk with your mouth full."

Shane grins. Dr. Overton can tell he's definitely more at ease with Matthew than with the others here. But who doesn't get along with Matthew? The kids' joy is infectious sometimes.

"So Shane," he attempts to change the subject again, not particularly interested in a theological debate with little ears listening, "Tell me a little about yourself. Sam and I haven't had much of a chance to talk so I'm not sure what all you've told her... but I'd love to hear a little more about your life and your people's ways."

"My people?" Shane looks confused at first and then clarity seems to hit. "Oh, yeah. My people... I don't really know what to tell you. President Smith was able to duplicate your vaccine and here we are."

"Do you have any family?" From his peripheral vision James notices his wife give him a 'slow down' look. But he ignores her.

Shane's face seems to sink and he looks pained for a moment. Then he slowly shakes his head and takes a bite of potato. After he swallows he sighs, "No. My parents... they didn't make it. But Cassie, I believe you know Cassie..." he pauses to give what seems to be a slightly accusing look before continuing, "She's been like a sister to me. Her mom died too, around the same time mine did. We've stayed together since. Looked after one another."

Maryanne's eyes swell with tears and she stands and moves with her plate towards the recycling bin. After she tosses it in she leaves the room without a second glance. Nobody at the table says anything for a moment or two.

"I'm so sorry to hear that Shane. Were the vaccines able to save many? I know the crowd we saw during the... well, you know... I don't imagine that was everyone right?"

Shane narrows his eyes. This line of questioning seems off somehow. "No... I mean, the vaccines saved quite a few of us. But mostly the younger generations. President Smith is one of the oldest that survived and she's only 43." He looks down at his plate again, it's almost clean now.

"We lost some of our elders as well. Their bodies couldn't adapt fast enough to the vaccine... I imagine those younger that were lost above probably had immune systems that couldn't fight off the radiation long enough for it to take effect... Again, I'm sorry. But I imagine you don't have much to fear these days anymore. Your weapons seem potent enough to fend off any living threat that may have survived and be out there. And I'm guessing you all have them. For protection?" Dr. Overton wipes his mouth with his napkin, trying to look casual despite his pounding heartbeat.

"I uh," Shane peers around him anxiously, "I think I'm done eating. I should check on Sam. Thank you for inviting me to lunch with you." He gets up and moves to place his tray where Maryanne had before. Then he quickly slips through the door before James could even think of an excuse to make him stay.

Chapter Twenty Six

When he arrives back at the infirmary he can see Sam is still sleeping. There's a nurse checking her vitals and making marks on a notebook. He slips in quietly and moves to Sam's side, brushing a stray hair out of her face. Her face scrunches up for a moment as if it had tickled her in her sleep. It's cute. Shane grins.

"How is she doing?" He addresses the nurse in a whisper.

The nurse glances up at him, then at Sam, and then back to her paper. "She's doing well actually. After that second dose she seems to be improving faster than expected. Of course, the sleep is probably helping a lot too. She seems to have an affinity with running off to get into trouble during the times she's meant to be resting. As I'm sure YOU are aware."

He nods, unsure how to respond to that. He sits by Sam's side for a while until a voice nearby catches his ear and he glances over at Andy's curtain. Through the thin opening he can see a woman inside talking with him, although he can't make out the conversation. After a moment the curtain pulls back and it's Kate that exits. She has a small vile of blood in her hand, Andy's probably. What could she need that for? Shane wonders. Kate makes eye contact with him and snarls, quickening her pace towards the door.

"Hey, wait!" Shane starts to yell after her and immediately regrets it when Sam starts to stir. The nurse, still nearby in the room, gives him an angry look and he puts his hands up apologetically before chasing after Kate. He pushes through the doors and calls to her again.

"Wait! Kate right? I wanted to..." he doesn't finish his thought before she whips around and sternly interrupts,

"No."

"No?" He tilts his head a bit, confused.

"No. My name. You and I are not on a first name basis nor will we likely ever be." She glares at him, her eye still dark from his people's assault on her. He never did hear an explanation for that. Not one that made sense anyway... President Smith is usually much more reasonable than that. He's still not sure what could have caused such a violent outburst.

"I'm sorry for what they did to you. It was wrong."

"You're dang right it was wrong! Everything your people do is wrong."

It takes everything in him to not get angry at such a comment. She doesn't even know his people... not enough to make such a claim anyway. But given the circumstances he tries to understand her frustration and keep his cool.

"You don't think it's wrong to hold the actions of a few against a whole people? Some of us weren't involved. I went to bat for you and I carried Sam home. Don't I deserve some good grace?"

Kate huffs but doesn't say anything. He can see in her eyes that she's thinking it over.

"I saw you with Andy. He's nearly healed from the acid rain. I've never thought that was possible. We've lost a handful of people to that rain over the years and had no defense but to run for shelter.

If y'all have created some kind of antidote..." he pauses to see her reaction. She remains silent. "You could save a lot of lives by sharing it with my people. I mean... it could wipe the slate clean after what happened five years ago."

He thought what he had to say was reasonable enough but apparently not. Kate's eyes seem to flare up in rage.

"Are you suggesting we owe your people anything? They are responsible for this!" She points at her eye before continuing, "and for Samantha's injury, and for Andy's arm! We provided your people with the vaccine four years ago. THAT should have wiped the slate clean. After that the only thing we expected, the only thing we owed your people, was peace." She turns and goes stomping off towards the staff only room. Shane sighs and begins to turn around himself when he catches her final words, barely loud enough to hear...

"And now we don't even owe them that."

Shane freezes, eyes widening. He spins back around to address the implications of what he may have just heard but Kate is already through the door, it clicking shut behind her.

Surely it wasn't anything. Maybe it was just her hurt talking. But a shiver runs down his spine as he makes his way back to Sam. Something tells him there's more going on around here than he's realized yet.

Moments later...

Back in the infirmary Shane checks on Sam. She's still asleep and he notices she's softly snoring a little. He considers sitting back down but the conversation with Kate keeps replaying in his mind. What had she meant? And what did she need Andy's blood for? If they already had a working vaccine then what else was there to do? His stomach twisted into knots. Maybe Andy would know something. He glances back towards Andy's curtain. Through a small opening he could see Andy was awake, reading a book of some kind.

Shane glances back down at Sam once more before quietly moving towards Andy. He slips through the curtain muttering, "knock knock" soft enough to hopefully not disturb Sam across the room.

"What's the point in saying knock knock if you intend to come in before receiving a response?" Andy whispers it, never looking up from his book. Shane tilts his head to read the cover. War and Peace. *Well that's old school...* He thinks to himself before responding to Andy's snide remark.

"Sorry. Didn't mean to interrupt. I was just curious about why, um, Kate needed a blood sample from you. I mean... it would seem the vaccine works." He nods towards Andy's arm. A mute gesture considering Andy still hasn't looked up at him.

"Interesting that you'd think I would know."

"Well, I just figured they'd have to give some explanation for why they were sticking you with another needle..." Shane struggles to control his annoyance.

Andy sighs and closes his book, a thumb still inside to hold his place, and finally makes eye contact with Shane. The moment his eyes land on him his expression changes to one of disgust. But as soon as it appears it's gone. Only a brief moment... but Shane had seen it. Honestly he wasn't sure whether to feel hurt or infuriated but he too did his best to hide his true feelings. There are more important things to worry about right now.

"I don't have any idea. The NASA staff here pretty much run things and we trust them to do what's best for us. She said they needed more of my blood so I said okay. That was basically it."

"There was no other comments or conversation? Even something small?"

The young man lying on the bed before him narrowed his eyes. "Well... I mean, she asked how I was of course. And then the reason we were out there when the rain hit to begin with might have come up briefly." Again, some disgust flashes across.

Shane tries to ignore it, "So... nothing more?"

"She said that never should have happened to me and it won't happen again. That's it." Andy shrugs and reopens his book in front of him.

"Hey, wait!" Shane pulls the top of the book down to see Andy's face again. "What did she mean though? Like how did she say it? Cheerful? Like, the vaccine will prevent it from happening again? Or..."

Andy huffs at him and pulls his book out from under Shane's hand. "I don't know! Seriously man can't you just..." then he pauses as if remembering something. "No. She wasn't cheerful. She was angry. And frankly most of us, really with Sam as the one exception, are. Honestly I wouldn't be surprised if Kate plans to get revenge somehow. It's not like it wouldn't be warranted. Now leave me alone."

Andy points towards the opening in the curtain, instructing Shane to exit. He does, shaking.

They are planning something. They have to be. He has to warn his people, and better yet, find a way to get some kind of peace treaty or something going before anyone else gets hurt. He rushes back to Sam's bed and begins hastily grabbing his dirty clothes and shoving them into a small, thin, plastic trash bag off the bin nearby. As he's tying the bag shut he hears Sam's voice behind him.

"Shane?" She's groggy from just waking up. "Is something wrong?" He turns back to her, what does he tell her?

"Um, no... I mean, I don't know. How are you?" He moves to her side and brushes his hand tenderly across her face again. She looks up at him, head tilted, super confused.

Oh yeah, he hasn't exactly expressed his recently expanded feelings for her yet... He really has no idea how to do that exactly. The world basically ending before he'd hit puberty didn't exactly allow for much time to figure these things out. And his loving gesture apparently comes across completely wrong because Sam's face turns to one of horror.

"Did someone die?! Oh gosh! Was it Andy?!" Her eyes get wide and he pulls his hand back in shock, especially at hearing Andy's name as the first one she'd be concerned about dying.

Somewhere in the back of the room, from behind Andy's curtain no doubt, comes a loud snort of amusement.

"What?! No! Nobody died! I just... look, I don't really have time to explain right now but I need to go back home and talk with President Smith. Everything's going to be okay. We can talk when I get back. We NEED to talk when I get back..." he grabs her hand and pulls it up to his lips, giving it a quick peck before turning and racing towards the door.

"What? Wait! Shane!" Shuffles and clangs ring out behind him but he doesn't look back as he pushes through the infirmary doors into the main lobby again.

Chapter Twenty Seven

I yank all the wires, tubes, and needles off of me and throw them back on the bed. My shoulder hurts and I wince, realizing I probably stretched it a bit too far pulling the iv out of the other. I start to chase after Shane but realize my hospital gown I'm now wearing is open in the back. The heat starts rising to my face and I groan as I reach back, grabbing the sheet off the bed to wrap around me. Once I've managed to tie it around me well enough I shuffle out as fast as my, probably still a little anemic from blood loss, body will allow.

The door is heavy and I have to lean on it to open it, again putting too much pressure on my arm and sending pain shooting through my shoulder.

"Ow! Shane! Wait!" I yell.

He's before me, heading towards the stairs, and to my right, my dad races towards him. To my surprise, he's trying to stop him as well.

"Shane! Listen to her! Stop! You can't leave!" He leaps in front of Shane and blocks his path. My dad grabs both of Shane's arms and holds him so he can't go around him.

"You can't keep me here like you did Cassie! Let me go home!" Shane fights against my dad's grip. He's pretty strong and if he applied his full force he probably could take my dad down honestly.

"I'm not trying to hold you hostage son! I'm trying to protect you dang it!"

At those words Shane goes still. His eyes narrow, "What do you mean? What did you do?!" He asks accusingly.

My dad looks taken aback and lets go of Shane's arms. "Do? It's raining again boy. Listen."

Shane looks up and so do I. The room gets quiet and sure enough, from up above our heads comes the soft 'clack clack clack' of rain hitting the metal ceiling.

"Oh..." Shane mutters. "Uh, thanks." He rubs the back of his head nervously.

"You're welcome." Dad then looks past Shane at me and shakes his head. "Samantha you really shouldn't be up. But so long as you are, why don't you find some clothes and you and Shane can join us for dinner in a bit."

A few minutes later in the women's restroom...

Have you ever tried to put on a t-shirt when you can't lift one of your arms without feeling excruciating pain? Let's just say, after about 10 minutes of trying my mom and I both decided it wasn't possible.

"Hang on a minute. I have an idea." Mom mutters before exiting the bathroom stall and rushing off.

I sigh and lean my head back against the concrete wall behind me, careful not to let my back touch it. I'm just standing there waiting in my strapless bra and blue jeans. But after just a moment she returns and knocks on the door for me to unlock it. I do and she slips inside quickly. She turns to me and holds up one of my father's royal blue button down shirts.

"That's going to swallow me." I inform her.

She huffs at me but instead of responding she just grabs my arm and begins pulling the sleeve of the shirt over my wrist. I try my best to wiggle in a way that makes it easier for her to get it up my arm without hurting my shoulder. Once we manage to get it on she begins to button it for me.

I was right. It hangs long and wide on my small frame. The sleeves alone come nearly an inch past my fingertips and the length reaches midthigh.

"Told ya." I gesture up and down myself as I turn to the mirror behind me. "It's like a really baggy dress on me..."

"Would you prefer the hospital gown that shows your bare behind?" Mom puts her hands on her hips and gives me a look.

"No..." I wouldn't but my voice doesn't exactly sound convincing. I look ridiculous and the thought of Shane seeing me like this doesn't seem appealing either. "It's just... I don't know."

I turn back to my mother and she looks thoughtful, "Hmm..." she breathes. "What about this?" She grabs the bottom of the shirt and unbuttons the bottom three buttons, stopping at the one nearest my waistline. Then she grabs the two unbuttoned sides and begins to tie them together, leaving what's left hanging down on either side.

I've got to admit, it's kind of cute this way. Trendy even.

"Wow, that's awesome mom! Thanks. Much better." I smile at her.

This is probably the first loving interaction we've had in a while. The thought causes my smile to waiver just momentarily but I put it back on as quickly as I can. She doesn't seem to notice.

"You're welcome. We should get to supper. I'm sure Shane will feel more comfortable with you there than he was during lunch without you..." she sighs.

"Lunch? What happened? Something I should know?" I tilt my head, a little concerned.

"Hm?" She asks, looking a little lost in thought. "Oh, no. I think he just felt awkward not knowing anyone is all. Let's go." She rushes out and I follow. It seems like she might be lying again. I shake my head. When does it end?

Once we exit the bathroom I notice Shane is standing outside the cafeteria shuffling his feet nervously. When he notices me walking up his eyes seem to shine with relief.

"Hey." He mutters.

"Hey, ready to eat?" I ask and he nods.

"Uh, you look nice..." His eyes graze over my unusual outfit and I try to force a smile. I'm not sure if he means it or if he's just trying to be nice. I feel like for what it is, a men's shirt two sizes too big, it's cute enough the way mom tied it up.

"Thanks. It was really the best we could do with my... arm." My eyes shift down, hoping I didn't make him uncomfortable by bringing up my injury. Thankfully it doesn't seem to bother him. "I like it. It's unique. Like you."

At that I blush a little. "Hey, what were you going to talk to me about? I mean, since you can't leave just yet, maybe we could talk now? And why were you wanting to leave so fast? What did I miss?" I lower my voice to ask but he shifts uncomfortably and shakes his head.

"Not here. Not right now. Maybe after dinner... if the rain hasn't stopped by then." He turns and holds the door open for me and I head on in.

Once inside I can smell the tangy scent of tomatoes and as we approach the counter to collect our tray I see why. Shane does too and his jaw drops.

"Spaghetti? Y'all have pasta?" He eagerly grabs a plate and we don't even make it to my family's table before he's already twirling it onto his fork.

"We grow the wheat and tomatoes. It's not like the canned stuff we grew up on but..."

"It's amazing!" He says ecstatically, right before slurping up another noodle. I giggle and we take our seats.

My dad raises an eyebrow at Shane's already halfway empty plate. "Well, I'm glad Maryanne already said grace before you got here."

Shane freezes mid bite and glances at me. I'm actually a bit confused myself considering my dad has never really been concerned about whether we say grace or not, that is until I see the look in his eyes. I smile and shake my head, turning back to Shane to let him know that dad is only teasing him. He swallows and announces, "Sorry, I just... spaghetti used to be my favorite food and it's just been a while. Thanks for letting me join you all again. And I'm sorry about earlier too... Thanks for stopping me." He nods appreciatively at my dad.

"It's alright. And you're welcome. You did seem to be in a hurry though. Was there anything wrong?" Dad scoops up another forkful of pasta but never takes his eyes off of Shane. I'm curious about the answer too but I doubt Shane gives one. Or at least not the true one...

"I uh, I've just been here a while and figured I should check in with Cassie is all." His eyes drift away from my dad and down to his plate again. Definitely a lie.

"I see." My dad mumbles it softly and I can tell he doesn't believe Shane either, but he makes no attempt to question him further.

We all eat in silence for a while until one of the other NASA staff rushes over and whispers something in my dad's ear. I catch only a bit here and there and not enough to piece together. But when I look over at Shane he looks concerned. Could he have heard more clearly? My dad turns back to face us and excuses himself from the table. My mom watches him go, looking as equally concerned as Shane does. After dad's gone Shane gets up too.

"I'm going to go ask if it's stopped raining yet." He explains and nods for me to follow. I do. My mom doesn't attempt to stop us.

I race out the door after him and see him making a beeline for the upper door.

"Wait! What if it's still raining?" I shout after him.

"It's not." He retorts.

"How do you...? Oh, Is that what they told dad?"

"Part of it." He reaches the door and carefully pushes it open, peeking outside.

"What was the rest?" I ask. He gets quiet. "Did you not hear the rest or..."

He twists his head back to look at me but hesitates before responding, "...I did." "Okay. And?" I pry.

"They took a sample of the rain." He looks nervous and I still don't understand.

"Your face suggests that's... a bad thing?"

He shakes his head and pushes himself out the door. I race up the steps and after him. Outside the sky is a light gray color to the east but sunny overhead. The ground is still wet and I briefly wonder if the wet ground would affect us if we were to walk on it barefoot. Not that I intend to test that out of course.

"They plan to weaponize it." His voice comes out soft with a twinge of fear. I almost can't believe I actually heard what I did.

"What? Are you sure that's what they said?"

"Positive. And we have to warn my people and come up with some kind of peace treaty before things get bad."

"I just can't believe my dad would... I mean... maybe they would make something like that but I don't think they'd use it unless it was absolutely necessary." I follow behind him closely as we head towards the wood line.

"I'm afraid in their minds they might already believe it is. After your shoulder." He doesn't look back at me when he says it. I'm glad because I just hang my head, realizing he may be right.

We make it to the middle of the woods between our two camps and a voice from the trees causes me to jump.

"Took you long enough."

I glance up above us to find Cassie in the tree, sitting on a branch with her back leaned against the trunk. She has something she's tossing around beside her. A yoyo?

"Cassie!" Shane's voice rises with excitement and she hops down from the tree. She wraps him in a hug and he squeezes her back.

"Glad to see they didn't kidnap you too." Her voice is playful rather than concerned. Then she turns to me as they pull apart, "and I'm glad to see you're alive and doing well. How's the kid?"

"Matthews fine. Thanks for carrying him." I mutter softly. She nods and turns back to Shane who addresses her before she can say anything else.

"Why are you out here?"

"Waiting for you. I figured you'd come out to update me eventually. Or I'd have to storm the gates and bust you out. I was gonna give it one more day before mounting a rescue."

Shane grins. "Thanks. I'm good though. But I need to talk with President Smith as soon as possible."

"Not the best idea." Cassie shakes her head. "Not sure we're still welcome after helping them. I mean, I've been back a time or two but I get some pretty interesting looks. I haven't tried getting close to her but I don't know that it would be an open door anymore."

"Well, it's important. I've got to try." He starts off in that direction and I start to move with him. Hearing my steps he whips around. "No. Sam, you have to stay here with Cass. I'll fill you in when I get back. I'm not risking losing you this time."

His words fill me with warmth and I nod. I don't let it show on my face but inside I'm gleaming. He really does care. My moment is short lived, however, when he turns back to Cassie.

"Be safe." She steps towards him and he towards her. I'm sure my face contorts in a "what the heck" expression as they lean in towards each other. But to my relief they don't kiss. But what they do is still odd to me and makes my stomach flop. Leaned in close, they each put their forehead up against the others. Not touching noses or lips, just foreheads, but it still feels strangely intimate and sends a shiver through me.

Shane runs off without another word and Cassie glances back at me. She seems to notice my disturbed demeanor and shakes her head before moving to sit against the bottom of the tree she was up in earlier.

"Don't worry. It's not what you think." She throws the yoyo again, letting it roll along the dirt before coming back to her. "We're just really close friends. More like brother and sister. We've been through a lot together."

"I didn't ask." I'm trying to play off my reaction but I know I'm failing at it.

"He's into you, you know?"

At this my back stiffens. "What?"

"You heard me. He has been since he found out you're alive the day y'all met again in the woods. But... something's changed now. I could tell the minute y'all walked up. I guess you almost dying is what he needed to realize how much he wanted you."

"He hasn't said anything to me..." I don't really know how to respond to any of this and I end up sitting down on the grass near her and just staring at her.

"Not surprising. He's never been good with expressing his emotions. I mean, neither am I. I'm probably worse really. But losing your parents young and having to fend for yourself can do that to a person. I'm sure he's just trying to find the right time."

I nod but I'm not really comfortable assuming anything about Shane's intentions. Although it seems if anyone would know him well enough to assume something like that it would be Cassie. I can't help but hope she's right. Maybe that's what he was wanting to tell me when he got back? You know, before the rain and before I ended up just coming with him.

"So," I start nervously, "How long do you think he'll be gone and when do you think we should start to worry?"

She glances off in the direction of their city and shakes her head.

"Good question." She mumbles.

Chapter Twenty Eight

"Welcome Shane. I assume you're here about your little yellow friend?" President Smith doesn't even glance up at him from the test tube she's messing with. "I'm sorry it came to that but I believe we made the consequences clear. Did she survive?" The vial on the table in front of her contains a blue liquid that bubbles and foams over the top. She holds it up to the light and mumbles to herself. "Drat." She huffs, placing it back down and turning his direction with a sigh.

"Yes. She did."

Doctor Carver finally looks up and nods. "You may or may not find me sincere when I say it but I am, in fact, happy to hear that. After all, it was never OUR intention to treat another group of people as disposable."

Shane's eyes narrow. "You're right, I don't find that sincere, but that's not actually why I'm here. Well, not exactly."

"Hmm..." she hums, as if uninterested. "Alright. Then what may I help you with?" She moves to a cabinet nearby and pulls out a Bunsen burner and another glass container.

"I believe the underworlders may be planning to get revenge for Sam's attack."

"Technically, her attack..." she makes quotation marks in the air with her fingers when she says 'attack' as she sets her items on the table, "was OUR revenge on their breaking the boundary rule. Which was put in place as revenge for their kidnapping of Cassie." "Which was their revenge for y'all's kidnap and assault on Kate." Shane accuses softly. The president shrugs.

"Which was our revenge for them leaving us to die in the first place. So again, it started with them. I'm a little curious if you've forgotten that... Where does your loyalty lie Shane?" She mixes some more chemicals and this time the mixture settles and there are no bubbles or foam. She grins triumphantly and places a cork in the vial.

"I'm not particularly thrilled about the idea of having to choose a side. The existence of sides indicates unrest. War even..." He shudders nervously and Dr. Carter glances at him in consideration before he continues. "And they did send us the antidote... does that count for nothing?"

The woman before him suddenly becomes angry, slamming her hands down on the table between them. Her eyes close and she breathes out heavily from her nose. He imagines if this was a cartoon there would be smoke coming out of her ears. She sighs deeply and her shoulders seem to relax slightly.

"Sure, they sent up one vial of antidote so they could act like our saviors when we wouldn't have been in that position in the first place if not for them. They brought us to this and then act like they are our heroes? No. We don't owe them anything. In fact, they ought to be on their knees begging for our forgiveness. But instead they are threatening war? Well, if they want a war we will give them one. Let them come." She holds up her vial to the light.

"President Smith, I have reason to believe they're making something that..."

"It doesn't matter." She interrupts him, "We will be ready. They think they are above us because of their fancy equipment but they aren't. We are not the uneducated and defenseless creatures they believe we are. And I would encourage you, Shane, to figure out which side of the tree line you want to be on before it's too late. Now if you would, see yourself out." She points to the door behind him with a stern look.

"But Doctor you just don't..." A large man enters the room and lays a hand on his shoulder. One of President Smith's security enforcers.

"You've been asked to see yourself out. Clearly you're struggling with that so allow me to direct you." He growls and instructs Shane out. President Smith has already returned to her work, ignoring them as they exit.

Chapter Twenty Nine

Seeing Shane walking back towards us just an hour or so later fills me with relief. I climb to my feet and rush to meet him. Cassie moves a little slower, calmly following behind. The look on Shane's face lets me know it didn't go well. Before I can say anything Cassie puts it into words.

"You look like you just had a door slammed in your face."

He glances over my shoulder at her and sighs hard. "Essentially."

I reach for his arm and rub it reassuringly. When my hand makes contact he seems to jump slightly, as if startled by my touch.

"What do we do now then? Talk to my dad?" I ask. He's looking at my hand on his arm but the question seems to draw his gaze back up to my eyes and he nods.

"We can try. But I'm thinking it won't matter anymore. I'm not sure there's a way to stop this." His tone is tired and sad. I have almost forgotten that Cassie is behind me when Shane addresses her again, "Oh, Cassie, if you don't want to come with us I think you're welcome to go back. I was given an ultimatum of sorts... but not completely rejected. I'm sure they'd let you go home without issue if that's what you want."

I turn around to Cassie, who appears to be thinking it over. "Okay. Yeah... no offense," her eyes meet mine when she says it, "but I'd rather go home. Or to the closest thing I have to one anyway." She moves around me and gives Shane a quick hug. Her head lingers by his ear a moment and I realize she's whispering something to him. His face goes a brownish shade for a moment and his eyes dart over to me. When he sees I've noticed he turns away again. Now the heat creeps into my cheeks as well. Gosh, I hope she isn't telling him anything I said while he was gone... When she pulls away she nods to me and runs back off in the direction of their community.

We start walking back to my base in awkward silence. But that doesn't last long. I begin to notice Shane grumbling to himself. He seems really irritated at whatever conversation he's replaying over and over again under his breath. I try to think of something to say to get his mind off of things, at least for the walk back.

"So... are there still bigger animals out here too? You know, like wolves?" I question, glancing around us.

"What?" I'm not sure he heard me over his own thoughts.

"Is everything that was here before still here? Just different? Like large animals that we should be concerned about?"

"Everything that was here before is still here." He mumbles. I'm about to ask another question but to my surprise he continues, "Nothing ever seems to change. Even the end of the world couldn't stop this stupidity."

Now I'm really confused. "Um, I'm guessing we aren't talking about wolves anymore?"

He shakes his head. "No. Well yes, wolves are still around too. And I guess in a sense I am talking about wolves... Human beings may as well be wolves sometimes. That human nature... That hate... It was here before and it's still here now. It just shifted from one thing to another. It's always been here and I guess it always will be."

I'm beginning to see where he's going so I try to go along with it.

"Well, what kept it at bay before all of this?"

"I don't know... A few people who didn't fall into the trap?" He stops walking a moment and seems to consider this.

"The trap?" I pause too, waiting for him to continue, both his walking and explaining.

"Yeah, hate. It's not like hating someone else hurts them. It just keeps you a prisoner inside yourself." The look on his face is so serious and I try to lighten the mood.

"Wow, deep." I laugh a little and Shane shakes his head.

"I'm serious though."

I feel a little bad for my chuckle now seeing how intense he is.

"Okay, well what drives out hate then?"

His eyes look deep into mine, "Love." He whispers softly.

I blush hearing the word escape his lips but I try my best to hide it from him. "Okay, so let's do that." I suggest as we start walking again.

Shane turns and raises an eyebrow at me, "Love?"

"Yeah, love."

.....

When we get back to the bunker everything is a buzz. I'm not sure anyone even noticed we were gone until dad walks out of the staff room and glares at me. His eyes narrow and he shakes his head.

"Sam, why do I even bother? You do understand I'm trying to protect you right?"

I don't respond. I just stare at him. He turns his attention to Shane.

"Young man, I'm going to give you some solid advice and I highly suggest you take it to heart. Unfortunately, I don't think these next few days are going to be pleasant. If you care for my daughter, or your own self preservation, I'd suggest you stay here with her and do not leave this bunker. Either of you."

He marches off towards the living quarters without further explanation. Shane turns to me, concern in his eyes. I don't say anything to him either. I head towards the staff door and bang on it, hard. Instead of just a crack this time, it flys wide open and Kate glares out at me, hands on hips.

"Your father isn't here." She growls.

"I know. I was looking for you."

"Why?"

"What's going on? And don't lie to me or try to send me to ask my dad. You know good and well he won't tell me because he thinks not knowing will protect me, or some kind of mess like that." I huff and stomp my foot a little, as if to declare how serious I am. She's unimpressed.

"You're right. Hiding things from you seems to only fuel your reckless behavior." She glances at Shane and scowls a moment before turning back to me, "There's going to be a war. It's starting tonight. You're going to need to stay out of it."

Shane and I lock eyes and the shared fear is on his face. Kate sees it too and shakes her head at him.

"I'm guessing the fact that you don't seem to have known is a good thing."

"How would I have known? Sure I suspected after our conversation earlier that y'all were planning something but..."

"We?" Kate laughs. "Yes Shane. We made a weapon to defend ourselves with just in case. But this war wasn't our decision. We just got this an hour ago via a giant bird again." She turns around and grabs a slip of paper from the table behind her and hands it to us.

Shane reads it silently and his face goes pale. He hands it back with trembling hands. "It's all my fault..." he mutters and backs himself up against a nearby wall before sliding down to the floor and placing his head in his hands. I hold my hand out and Kate lets me see the note.

Given the circumstances prior to this, and the fact that we have been made aware of malicious intent, we see no other option but to defend what has become our land and our home. We are

prepared to fight for our lives and this time we will have the upper hand. Consider this our declaration of war. Surrender now and leave or be prepared to meet us at night fall at the halfway point between our camps.

Sincerely, The Overworlders

I sigh and return the note. Kate nods to me and closes the door. I turn and lower myself to the floor in front of Shane. I'm sitting on my knees and I lean forward, lifting his head up to see his face. "Hey, we knew it was coming eventually. It's not your fault."

"Made aware of malicious intent. They sent the message right after I left. I'm the one who made them aware of the weapon..."

"They used that as their excuse to declare. But they would have found a reason without it. Their hearts are hardened. Both sides. They were looking for a reason to fight. They didn't need us to find one for them." I take his hands in mine and he looks at them as if deep in thought. "Besides, we had a plan right? To fight against this with love?"

He stares at me solemnly. "I don't even know what that means."

My heart sinks a little, "You don't know what love means?"

He shakes his head, "No, I mean, I know what love means. At least, I think I do... now that... um..." He goes quiet and looks at me deeply for a moment. My heart starts beating faster. Suddenly he shoves his head forward and his lips meet mine. I freeze, unsure of what to do. I've never been kissed before and even though I've been waiting for this moment, now that it's here, I have no idea how to kiss him back. The moment I start to try, he pulls back before I can.

He looks embarrassed. "Sorry... I just..."

I shake my head, "No, it's okay... I mean, more than okay, I mean... sorry I didn't kiss back. I don't really know how." My face grows hot and I glance around to see if anyone noticed the awkward exchange. There are a lot of people moving quickly through the room but none seem to be looking our way or interested. Thankfully.

"Okay." He mumbles, unsure.

I feel bad and suggest, "Maybe we could try that again?" He nods and this time I lean in. We kiss, and while it's still awkward and a little disorganized, it's definitely better.

"I'd suggest maybe the third time's the charm," I grin, "but we should probably deal with what's going on..."

He smiles warmly and brushes some hair from my face. "Yeah, what I meant though, is that I don't know how to fight a war with love."

"Oh, yeah. Well, if the two sides hate each other, but we are from opposite sides and we love each other..." I mention it and his face gets a little darker, "then what if we show the other side that it's possible? That even though we are different we care about them and their lives too? We go tonight and address the two sides before they start. Try to reason with them and explain that love is better?"

"And if they don't listen and they start shooting each other anyway?"

"Then... then we prove it with our actions and do everything we can to protect them and stop them."

"Or we die trying?" He raises an eyebrow as if to suggest the likelihood of that happening.

I nod. "I think I'm willing to risk it. My life to save hundreds? I can't think of any bigger expression of love... If that's what it takes to change hearts... Would you agree? Or am I just crazy?"

"You're crazy."

I hang my head but he lifts it up and continues. "But you might not be wrong. If you're willing to go that far for my people, then I'm willing to do the same for yours. We're in this together."

Moments later...

"Remind me again why we need in there?" Shane whispers behind me as I watch the door to the NASA control room. Several people have exited it already including my father; all heading outside to prepare for battle.

"To get the antidotes. The one for the regular rain and the one for the weaponized rain they made for the war. We might be able to negotiate with your side by offering them the rain antidote." "And if that doesn't work?" He questions.

"Then we may need the other to save their lives."

"What about the weapon President Smith created? We won't have the antidote for it to save your people..."

"Well, we will just have to hope that by making the first move ourselves that she'll have a change of heart and help us too." I hold up my hand to stop him from responding as the door swings open again. Two more men leave and I do some quick figuring in my head and nod to Shane. "That's the last of them. Let's go." We walk towards the door and stand near it casually. I signal for Shane to look out for anyone as I pull the key card from my back pocket. He raises an eyebrow at me.

"Where did you get that?"

"It's Kate's. I snatched it off her while we were talking with her in the doorway earlier. She was distracted when she was giving you the note and smarting off to you. It was sticking out of her back pocket and I grabbed it." I shrug as if it's no big deal but to be honest the thought of what I'd done still makes my stomach churn. That's never really been who I am but... desperate times and all.

His look appears both impressed and concerned but he doesn't say anything. I swipe it and push the door open a crack, glancing inside carefully to make sure I was right about the count. I was. It's empty. We rush inside letting the door click shut behind us.

The room is full of tables, all of which are covered in various equipment and papers. Along the walls are different storage drawers and containers, some fancier and others more old school. The back wall is covered in computer screens, buttons, and blinking lights.

I move to a containment area along the right wall. Inside the glass there are vials filled with different colored liquids.

"I think this is it!" I call to Shane. He walks over and examines the clear box before nodding. He points at the keypad on the front. There's a small slit in the front of the keypad and I shove Kate's card into it, hoping that's what it's for. It must be because the box makes a noise, the dome top opens up, and the three drawers under the dome all move forward slightly, unlocking for us to pull them out further if we choose.

"Are they labeled?" He asks. I pull one out of the dome area at the top. The vial has a small white sticker on the front which reads RAD29-U. I nod. "What's that one?"

I place it back and pull out the next drawer. "That one's the original vaccine for the radiation."

"So do you know the names of the two we need?"

"No. But as far as I know they haven't made any more than those three. I'd imagine these last two drawers are the ones we are looking for." I pull a vial out of each of the other slots and hold them up to the light to look at them. One is pinkish and the other is a light orangey color. The pink one is labeled 'RRR-V32' and the orange is labeled 'RRR-DW32'.

"One vial wouldn't be enough though right?" He questions, looking at the two in my hands.

"Probably not..."

"So how do we carry them?" Shane moves across the room and starts searching through drawers for something useful. After a minute he mumbles, "hmm," he holds up a small tray with circular holes and a plastic lid. "Found something." He brings it over and we start filling it, half with one vial and half with the other. Suddenly there's a loud CLANK noise behind us. I spin around, concerned.

"What was that?!"

Shane gets quiet as if listening. "Not sure. Came from the door I think."

I race back over to the door and swipe the card. It makes a noise but doesn't unlock. My eyes widen in fear. "Shane!" It's apparent that the tone of my voice causes him to worry too and he rushes over with the now full carton of tubes.

"We're locked in." I whisper. I turn back to the door and start banging on it and shouting. "Hey! Hey! In here! The door is stuck!" From the other side of the door comes a voice.

"It's not stuck. Did you really think it would be that easy to get Kate's card? Honestly Sam..."

Confusion fills me. "Andy?"

"Yes. I'm sorry Sam. Your dad instructed us to make sure you didn't leave tonight. It's for your own safety."

"Andy! Listen! This isn't right! We can stop all of this and make peace. We need to love one another! We are all human beings! Let us out! We can fix it!"

"Goodbye Sam." Andy's voice sounds further away, and the footsteps fade off into the distance.

"Andy!" I slam my fists against the door in anger. "Ugh!!!" I turn back to Shane and slink to the floor. He kneels down and plants himself beside me, setting the tray on his other side.

"Well, on the bright side. I guess your dad's warming up to me if he trusts me locked in a room alone with you all night." He grins and I shove him gently.

"Not funny." I mutter, leaning my head back against the door and sighing.

We sit there in silence several minutes before a faint sound on the other side of the door draws my attention.

"Did you hear that?" I ask Shane. But before he can even respond a small voice finds its way through the metal door.

"Sammy?"

I squeal with delight and leap to my feet, planting my ear against it. "Matty?!"

Shane stands up beside me and picks the vials up off the floor.

"Sammy, I saw Andy lock you in there. That was mean."

"Yes, it was very mean. Can you help us get out?"

"I don't know. There's a thing on the door."

"What kind of thing? What does it look like?" I ask.

"Um, it has buttons and the buttons have numbers and letters on them."

I turn to Shane. "Numbers and letters. Probably like an old cell-phone? You think?" He nods in agreement and I turn my attention back to Matty outside the door.

"Okay Matty, is there a screen with blank spaces?"

"Yeah!"

"How many? Can you count them?"

"One. Two. Three. Four. Five. Six. Seven. Eight! There's eight!"

"Okay. Great. Thanks Matty. Um, try this Matty, 101213." Matty begins pressing buttons as I turn to Shane who gives me a curious look. "My parents' wedding date." He nods as if to say "oh okay." Beeps come from the other side but no clicks.

"Didn't work Sammy."

"Okay... um..." I start and Shane cuts in.

"What if it's your name?"

"What?"

"I don't know. I've read books like that before. Turns out to be the kid's name or something."

"That's a bit cliche for my dad..."

"Never know."

"Fine. Matty, try my name. But not Sammy okay? Samantha. S. A. M. A. N. T. H. A." A moment later, the same beep. I give Shane an 'I told you so' look and he shrugs.

"Worth a shot." He mutters.

"Oh! I know! Matty, try 042533!" I tap on the door excitedly. "I'm like 90% sure that'll be it."

Shane shakes his head, "We better hope so. What if this thing won't let you try more than 3 times in like a certain amount of time?"

"This has to be it. I'm sure. It's the date we came out of the bunker. Immersion Day."

"It's also the date of your 18th birthday. What if he chose it for that reason? Then I would kind of be right wouldn't I?" He pokes fun but I just ignore him, head against the door waiting to hear if I'm right.

There's a beep and a screech as the door begins to open. "Yes!" I shout and leap for joy. "I knew it! I knew it!" As the door swings open I prepare to give Matthew a big hug, "Thanks bud! I knew you could..."

I go silent and slowly lift myself back up, pulling my arms in against myself from their 'hug ready' position.

The person standing before me taps their foot in disapproval.

"Um, hey mom..." I whisper.

"Samantha Rose. Honestly?"

"So... was I right about the code?" I ask curiously despite her glare. She sighs.

"No. You weren't. Do you want to know what the code was?"

I nod. Shane is wisely standing back, silent as a mouse during this confrontation.

"The code was 043028."

"The day we came in here?!" My jaw drops. I try to make sense of why my father would choose such a horrific date as his code. "That's sick..." I mutter.

Mom's eyes narrow. "Your father chose that day because of his guilt. He feels so bad for not saving those other people, despite knowing it wouldn't have been possible, that he chose to make that code that date to essentially punish himself with shame everyday. Your father is not the monster you believe him to be Samantha. But he is lost. I hope you can get through to him. Now go. Do what you plan to do. I pray it works."

She steps aside and motions for us to go. We do. But as we run, tears well up in my eyes. I wipe them away and as my hand falls back to my side Shane wraps it in his.

Chapter Thirty

When we arrive in the clearing both groups are already there, but thankfully no violence has yet ensued. The two sides stand about thirty yards apart, facing one another. I can hear both my father's voice, as well as the voice of a woman. They sound angry. Shane's jaw is set sternly as he listens. We come at the two groups from the side, running directly into the gap between them. Shane faces the overworlders as I face my father and his "army" of my fellow underworlders.

Shane still has the carrier of vials in his hands and my dads eyes narrow at it before turning back to meet mine.

"I see you escaped. And stole from me in the process." I glance behind me at Shane who doesn't turn around. But over his shoulder I notice the woman, President Smith no doubt, staring at the vials intrigued. Shane must have noticed as well because he tightens his grip on the holder and moves it an inch or two behind him.

"Stole what?" Dr. Carter questions. Her voice is dripping with a fake sweetness. It reminds me of what a snake would sound like if it could talk. A tempting voice that pulls you in, giving you a false sense of security, when really it has every intention of doing you harm.

I ignore her. So does everyone else.

My attention is back on my father now. "Is stealing with the intention to save lives a worse offense than the reason you came here today?"

"Saving lives how? What is that?!" Smith's honey dipped tone is gone, replaced by a firm, and almost desperate, demand for an answer. Again she's ignored.

"You don't know what you're talking about." Says my father, frustrated. "We have to do what we have to do to survive. They can't be trusted as our neighbors. They aren't like us!" The moment the words escape my father's lips a rumble of voices surge through the crowd of overworlders behind me.

Shane steps backwards, his back now touching mine. I glance behind me to see Dr. Carter Smith slowly inching towards him, her eyes still glued to his hand with the vial holder. "That's some kind of medicine isn't it. An antidote? For what? Let me have it Shane!" She demands as her steps get quicker. Shane tries to back up further but now my father is lunging for us as well; both leaders desperate to get their hands on the carrier.

Shane grabs my arm and attempts to run with me but I resist. "STOP IT! Both of you! We need to come to an agreement! It doesn't have to be this way! We are all human beings and we should all treat each other as such!" I scream at them but it has no effect. President Smith reaches us first and attempts to dive for the container in Shane's hand.

I try to grab her arm to hold her back, yelling for her to just listen to us first. She's too strong and her eyes are filled with furious determination. Her arm is ripped away from my grip and her elbow makes contact with my nose, giving off a sickening THWACK!

A scream rises up in my throat and I try my best to hold it in... but I can't. The shrill shriek escapes as I drop to my knees and reach for my nose. When I pull my hand away it's covered in blood. My eyes go wide, but not because I'm hurt... I look up and my fears are confirmed. As Shane continues to try to reason with and fight off the president, who doesn't even seem to have noticed what her unintentional assault has caused, my father has stopped running and is staring at me intensely. His gaze follows the line of blood pouring out of my nose, staining my shirt red.

His eyes fill with what can only be described as pure hatred. He releases an animal-like howl of anger ending in the call I was trying so hard to prevent.

"ATTACK!"

As the cry bellows out of my father's mouth I try desperately to interject.

"No! Dad, stop! I'm fine! Don't do this! Call them off!" but it's too late.

The rumble of feet, the blasts of bullets, and the cries of War... it's all too loud for anyone to hear anything anymore. And honestly, the hatred ringing in their own ears would probably drown everything else out regardless. Then, to make matters worse, out of the corner of my eye I watch as Shane gets overtaken and Dr. Carter runs off into the woods with the vials. Shane attempts to chase after her but is confronted by another one of his people.

"Oh no you don't, traitor!" The man spits.

Shane huffs, annoyed, as he tries to sidestep his combatant only to be shoved back. "I don't want to fight you man! I'm trying to save all of us!"

The man won't listen and leaps on him. I turn my head from them to the woods nearby and notice my father and Kate racing after the President. I hop to my feet. My nose still hurts but I have to stop this. Thankfully the gushing has quit, leaving nothing but a blackish red trail of dried blood staining my face. I probably look like I just crawled out of one of those old cage fight things but I don't exactly have the time to go wash up when lives are literally on the line.

My feet thud heavily through the trees as I push myself as hard as I can to catch up with them. I can't remember the last time my heart beat this fast. My breaths get shorter and shorter which makes my face hurt even worse, but I push on through the pain. Finally, up ahead is a small clearing with a cliff overlooking what appears to be at least an 80 foot drop.

Near the edge I spot my father and the president. President Smith stands about fifteen feet from my dad, her back to me and facing him, with some kind of dart wielding weapon in her right hand, pointed at his face. It looks to be some kind of makeshift handheld crossbow. Her other arm lay slightly behind her, holding the container of vials. One of them appears cracked and is slowly dripping on the dirt beside her. I'm not sure what ensued before I arrived to damage the vials but apparently something did. I start to step out of the shadows towards them but what she says next stops me in my tracks.

"Oh sure. Now you want to negotiate. Now that I have the upper hand and it's your own skin on the line. What about when it was my peoples lives at stake?"

Her voice sounds almost deranged but her hand remains steady on her weapon. I'm surprised to hear that my dad was trying to negotiate at all. That's what I'd been begging him to do this whole time and he'd just kept refusing despite the consequences. What changed? Dr. Carter seems to think he's doing it out of self preservation... But my father has always been a very strong, very proud, man. I can't see him rolling over on anything he believes in for just his own sake. Had he finally thought about what I'd said? Had he finally realized that hate wasn't the answer? Maybe he...

But as the thoughts race through my mind, something catches my attention. My father's left hand behind his back. He flicks his fingers in an odd pattern. With a fist made he brushes his thumb over his pointer finger from one end over to the other, repeatedly. This motion confuses me. A nervous tick maybe? But I've never seen him do it before...

I glance around the tree line near the edge of the clearing and that's when I see it. A glint from the sun reflecting off a metal surface. A gun, and behind the gun, Kate.

~~~~~

Shane rolls around with the gruff man, leaves crunching beneath them. The occasional stick pokes into his back but it's nothing compared to the fists raining down against his chest and face. Finally the weight on him abruptly shifts and he gasps for breath, glancing around frantically to see where the man went and if he should expect a further assault. Off to his left he can see them.

"Not you too!" The man grumbles, shaking his shaved head in disbelief.

He's addressing Cassie, who apparently had been the one to drag him off of Shane.
~~~~~

She sighs, "Nobody is a traitor here. You need to look at the bigger picture. The greater good."

Her words aren't going over well but at least he seems more apt to talk with her than he did with Shane before. As Cassie distracts the man, Shane pulls himself quietly to his feet and stumbles off into the woods to catch up with Sam.

It's not hard to find their trail and track them down once he's on his way. He's been learning to track for survival for years now. When he comes to the clearing he bursts through it, following the voices and images of bodies up ahead. There was no pause or hesitation in exposing himself from the treeline but even so he finds himself just moments too late. Shane watches in horror as the scene before him unfolds, almost as if in slow motion:

Sam racing across the clearing towards Dr. Carter, her arms thrusting forward and shoving the President to the ground, a simultaneous gunshot ringing out, Sam's body falling through the air but suddenly jerking backwards as the bullet hits her shoulder, and her body disappearing over the cliff's edge.

His heart stops. He tries to scream her name but his voice catches in his throat. *This can't be real*, he thinks. *It can't be.*

Epilogue:

Have you ever done a cannonball into the deep end of a swimming pool? Do you remember the water sucking you down, maybe

faster and further than you originally anticipated; and the slight pressure as your body makes contact with the bottom? Then you look up and for a brief moment your mind contemplates the idea that the distance to safety might be too great. You feel a slight sense of concern bubble up in your chest as you begin to push yourself off the floor and kick furiously towards the surface. And the closer you get to it, the tighter your chest becomes. But then you burst out of the water as if being violently yanked through a portal to another dimension and you gasp for breath as you're hit with a rush of emotions. Relief, excitement... But also a touch of lingering fear, a reminder that what you just experienced could have killed you... But didn't.

That's what it felt like right before I opened my eyes.

The bullet hitting me and my body falling off the cliff was jumping in the water. Freefalling was the tightening in my chest as I fought for the surface. Hitting the ground, which I really don't remember actually happening, but I have to assume it did, was bursting through that imaginary portal.

And waking up to find it had all been a dream...

That was the end result. A gasp of breath, relief, excitement... And a touch of lingering fear.

I peer around my room. Nothing has changed. I glance down at myself. Tan skin. No yellow. I climb out of bed and make my way to the window. The sun is just coming up. That must mean the world is safe after all...

I stare out the glass pane at the yard. The grass is wet with dew and a few birds peck at it. Normal birds. Normal grass. Normal sky.

Everything is back to normal. But I don't feel normal anymore. I almost miss the world in my dream. Even though, had it been real, that world was about to end for me anyway. The strange thing is... if given the option to do anything in the dream over again... I wouldn't change anything. Not even if it hadn't been a dream.

I know that fearing death is normal. Most people, given the foreknowledge of how they will die, will attempt to change their path and ultimately their end. But I don't think that's what I would have wanted in the dream. Because my death had a greater purpose. A saying comes to mind, a memory of something I'd read or heard, that "there is no greater love than to lay down one's life for someone else." That may not be the exact wording but I'm fairly sure that's what it boils down to.

Shane and I, well our dream selves, had made this plan to bring peace and unity through love. And if I understand the saying correctly... my saving the president, even at the cost of my own life... well maybe that's the kind of love it was going to take. Nothing else would have worked. Nothing less than complete sacrificial love that puts others above ourselves can stop hate. Especially a hate that sees ourselves as ultimately worth more than others for any reason.

I walk back to my bed and sit on the edge. What if I were to go back to sleep? What would happen? Is there any realm of possibility in which I might be able to see the aftermath of my sacrifice? Like an out of body experience where I can watch the rest of the dream play out from above? I want to know if hearts were softened and minds were changed. I want to know if the two groups could learn to see each other not by their skin or their past mistakes but by their souls and by their capacity for love. But I know I'm asking a lot of a dream, even a magnificently realistic one.

My phone buzzes somewhere behind me and I reach for it. The screen lights up, 6:25 am. A notification on my lock screen informs me that I have a new message.

Shane's name pops up on the screen followed by: "If you get to school in time for breakfast we should eat together and work on our project. I'm glad we got teamed up for it. I can't help but think we'd make a good pair..."

A faint smile tugs at the edges of my lips. Somehow, I think he's right.